MW00608533

WALLFLOWER
BLOOMING

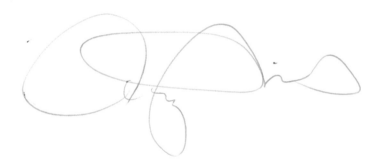

WALLFLOWER BLOOMING

Amy Rivers

WPP

WOODEN PANTS PUBLISHING

Printed in the United States of America
First Printing, 2016
Wooden Pants Publishing

Cover image used under license from shutterstock.com

ISBN-10: 0997353562
ISBN-13: 978-0997353563

CHAPTER 1

Val Shakely was at a proverbial standstill. The world turned; she went about her life in an orderly and systematic way. But at some point, she'd gotten stuck. And she was happy to stay stuck. It was uncomplicated. If you stayed stuck, life would wash around you, like water around a boulder in the middle of a river. You could hide yourself in plain sight.

As Val walked toward the restaurant, she savored her last few minutes of calm. She was meeting her cousin Gwen, and Gwen never stood still.

Despite being busy professional women, Val and Gwen were close, and a formal dinner date was a special occasion. When Gwen insisted they meet at The Vine, one of Cambria's most upscale restaurants, Val figured something big was up. Sure enough, when they sat down from each other, Gwen bounced on her seat, practically bursting with excitement.

"I'm going to do it, Val," she said, her smile so big the creases in her cheeks looked almost painful.

Of course, Val knew immediately what "it" was. Gwen had involved herself in local politics ever since she'd returned to Cambria after college. While Val built a public relations firm, Gwen had won a hotly contested seat on the city council. Now, she'd decided to throw her hat into the mayoral race.

Can't you just get married or have a baby like other women our age, Val thought, immediately feeling like a huge hypocrite. After all, it's not like she'd done either of those things, and she had a few years on her cousin.

"And," Gwen continued, with a twinkle in her eye, "I know I can do this because I'll work with *the* best, most effective public relations firm in town – yours!"

Aha, the real reason for the dinner date. Val sighed as her mind raced through the implications of taking on Gwen as a client. A big *NO* ached to come out of her mouth, but in deference to her cousin, she held it back. She'd known the request would come ever since Gwen first considered running, and Val had dreaded it.

Val had a bad history mixing politics and business. As a result, she'd assumed a firm stance against taking on those clients. But this was Gwen! How could she say no to the one person who'd stuck with her through thick and thin? Her stomach turned while considering her options.

"I don't know, Gwen. I'm not big on the idea of putting the business in the middle of politics in this town." Val shifted uncomfortably in her seat.

Gwen flashed Val a knowing look but soldiered on, determined to get her way. "What? You mean you won't help me? Don't you have confidence in me?" Gwen asked, playing on Val's loyalty and faith in a way she understood would hit the mark.

Val groaned. There was a reason why Gwen succeeded in politics, and not only due to her girl-next-door good looks, as her opponents would have people believe. When Gwen wanted something, she never gave up.

"Of course I do, Gwen. You know me better than that, so stop being an obnoxious brat." Val threw her cousin a mock glare and assumed a more serious expression. "Let's talk about this realistically. This can turn into a disaster for several reasons, not the least of which is Mayor Barton. You and I both know he won't let it slide, that I refused to take him on as a client in the last election, if I turn around and help my cousin in this one."

Val's refusal infuriated Roger Barton. Not used to being denied a request, he clearly couldn't believe Val's tiny firm would decline to take his business. Though Val abhorred confrontation, Barton's arrogance had made it much easier for her to say no. He'd vented his frustration publicly, and the stress of even that much attention on Val firmed her resolve. She knew for certain involvement in Gwen's campaign would develop into a nightmare.

"Barton hates you anyway, so who cares what he says now? Besides, I'm not asking you to volunteer. I want you to do marketing … to officially represent my campaign. I'm not looking for an endorsement, just your services." Gwen smiled sweetly, batting her eyelashes at Val in the particular way she did when she went for the kill.

Val knew Gwen had won, and her heart pounded so hard it made her head throb. She hadn't been able to say no to Gwen on past occasions, and it looked like this wouldn't be the first time. Reluctantly, she resigned herself to the inevitable.

"Alright, Gwen. Fine."

Gwen squealed, moved quickly around to Val, and gave her an overly enthusiastic hug which made Val gasp for breath.

"I knew you'd come around." Gwen grinned sheepishly.

"If I'm going to do this, you have to promise me something," Val continued, letting her uncertainty go for a moment to reveal a hint of the feistiness people rarely saw. "Promise me you'll win, Gwen, because I'm not sure I can deal with Barton if you lose."

Val managed an uneasy chuckle. She sipped her wine and settled in for what became a strategy session.

Gwen had come fully prepared for Val to say yes. She handed her a stack of papers outlining her campaign plans, budget, marketing ideas, and a painfully detailed overview of Barton's time in office. It also contained all the details which Gwen assumed Barton would try to use against her.

By the end of dinner, Val was sick with anxiety. The next day, she sent contracts to Gwen's office, and before lunchtime, her firm represented the Gwen Marsh for Mayor campaign.

* * *

Name officially added to the ballot, Gwen threw a campaign kick-off party. Val, who preferred jeans, reluctantly dusted off a little black dress for the occasion. She walked into the ballroom at the Hyatt Regency, and her cousin's supporters nearly trampled her. The room swarmed with activity. She looked around for Gwen but couldn't see her among the throngs of people.

Val had to admit awe at the turnout. Gwen had been an active and controversial city councilperson for the last four years, known for her unwavering commitment to governmental transparency. She helped rewrite municipal election guidelines limiting campaign contributions by corporate donors to create what she considered a more even playing field. This gained her more than a few enemies, such as Barton and other council members.

A server offered Val a glass of wine which she gladly accepted, and she inched toward the front of the ballroom, stopping to greet people she knew.

Val loved her cousin's stance on campaign finances, and that she had won her coveted council seat based on blood, sweat, tears, and little money. Refusing to accept corporate donations, Gwen's campaign budget was approximately one-hundredth of her opponents', but she'd won anyway. Working with her on this mayoral campaign would give Val a chance to make a further impact in the community.

She made it about mid-way through the room when she glanced over and noticed a man in a black suit with a pink tie nearly identical in color to her purse. *Brave*, she thought.

Almost on cue, the man's head tilted up and met Val's. Realizing she'd been caught staring, she smiled nervously, pointed at her purse, and gestured at the tie. He looked familiar to Val, but she couldn't place him.

He smiled back, eyes sparkling with amusement, and returned to a conversation the men surrounding him appeared to be enthralled with. As Val continued to wade across the room, the man pointed at her, and several of his companions turned to look. She could sense her face grow hotter. She tucked her head and pushed her way through the crowd and out of their line of sight.

Someone caught her arm. "Val, you look like a beet!" Gwen said, keeping a tight grip as they moved over to one corner of the room. "Do you feel alright?"

"I'm fine." Val took a deep breath and attempted to push the embarrassing moment out of her mind. "Looks like you're a hit."

"Even I'm surprised by the turnout." Gwen giggled, gesturing toward the crowd and sounding lightheaded from the wine. "Did you notice that gaggle of suits over there?" She pointed in the direction of Val's mystery man.

"Yep. The ringleader's tie matches my purse." Val glanced back but couldn't find the right position to see the gentleman from where she stood.

"That's John Hatfield," Gwen said, matter-of-factly.

Val nearly spit out her wine and ended up sputtering and coughing, her face shifting from red to a pale purple as she struggled for air. Gwen, looking alarmed, hit her hard on the back.

"Don't beat me up!" Val half laughed and half winced as the wine stung the inside of her throat. Once she'd regained most of her composure, she said, "John Hatfield? You've got to be joking."

"Nope. My staff sent him an invite. I had no idea he'd actually show up."

John Hatfield was something of a business legend in town as head of Hatfield Paper Products. He rarely made public appearances. In fact, Val had invited him to a half-dozen charity events and had received a polite refusal from his secretary every time. Looking in the general direction of the suits, Val pondered the man.

"I'm somewhat shocked he actually exists." Val hoped her cool tone covered her true emotions as her face started to burn again. She wondered how ridiculous she'd made herself in front of one of the most influential men in Cambria if not Colorado. She coughed a few more times. Beads of perspiration formed on her forehead, and she felt queasy.

"I think you should take it easy on the wine," Gwen said, misinterpreting the shade on Val's cheeks.

"I need to get some air." Val put down her glass, excused herself, and walked toward the ballroom entrance in search of some water or possible escape – it was a toss-up.

She spied a table with water bottles, scooped one up, and pried the cap off. She took several hurried gulps and relished the delicious cold liquid as it hit her irritated throat.

Someone brushed against her back. Val turned, and nearly ran face first into John Hatfield.

"Are you okay?" he asked, smiling. Val could hear amusement in his calm, smooth voice.

"Yes, except that you practically knocked me over," Val mumbled, though he had barely touched her. She hated being taken off guard, so she sounded more annoyed than she felt. John stood claustrophobically close. For the second time, Val wished she'd stayed home.

She studied him. His eyes seemed puffy, like he needed a good night's sleep, but he was still attractive. Handsome. In fact, downright gorgeous in a brooding sort of way. And coming to the realization increased her frustration with the situation, though she couldn't figure out why.

"I'm John," he said, casually.

"Val … Shakely," she stuttered, not her finest moment.

"You own the PR firm representing Ms. Marsh, right?"

"Yes. Are you going to follow her campaign?" The question

sounded ridiculous. After all, she knew the rarity of his public appearances, so he must have made this exception for a reason.

"Actually, yes," he said rather seriously. "I'm particularly interested in how she intends to win without a nickel to her name"

Val found herself getting defensive. "Money doesn't make a good candidate, Mr. Hatfield. Gwen works hard, and she's committed to this community."

"So, you recognize me?" he smirked. He smirked! *Who smirks? Movie villains?*

"Of course I do. I've lived here all my life. Anyway, I thought we were talking about Gwen."

Val shifted uncomfortably. She despised participating in political campaigns and here she was, in front of a local business mogul, feeling totally intimidated, embarrassed, and flustered. She couldn't pinpoint what made her so hostile toward him, but she could feel the conversation shifting in a bad direction.

Before John had a chance to say anything further, Val's sense of self-preservation finally kicked in. "Mr. Hatfield, it was a pleasure to meet you. I hope you'll forgive me, but I'm not feeling well." Without another word, she turned and walked out the door.

* * *

Back in the safety of her apartment, Val breathed a huge sigh of relief and chastised herself. *Well, I doubt he'll be donating to my causes now.*

She kicked off her shoes, poured a glass of water, and plopped down on the sofa. She flipped on the television and groaned as an image of Gwen and John Hatfield popped up on the screen. A quick look at her watch told her the party would continue for some time. She turned up the volume to hear John say, "… speaking with Ms. Marsh's PR representative tonight, and I've taken a particular interest in this campaign."

Val crinkled her nose. She couldn't think of a thing she'd said which would have made any significant impact on the man.

She'd been rude and defensive, not her most shining demonstration of professionalism. Once again, Val chided herself for getting involved in her cousin's campaign.

She reviewed her interaction with John. She paused on his screen image and stared into the dark, brooding eyes that held a glimmer of amusement, giving him an unmistakable air of smugness. She found him extremely attractive. Even thinking about him from the safety of her couch made her strangely uncomfortable.

Why did a man she'd barely met and would likely never see again make her feel so off-kilter? It was probably the not knowing. Val saw herself as a straightforward individual who wore her emotions on her sleeves. She kept her life as simple as possible, and uncertainty made her uneasy, so she tended to avoid things she couldn't control or take charge of.

In all of Val's dealings in Cambria, she and John never crossed paths, at least not in person. Relief filled her when she realized the chances of seeing him again were so slim. Head resting comfortably on the back of her couch, Val closed her eyes and dozed.

* * *

Val woke up feeling perky, ready for the day. On her way to the office, she grabbed coffee and a breakfast burrito from her favorite local dive and exchanged greetings with Harry, the restaurant's owner. *The usual*, she thought, contentedly, the familiar weight of the bag in her hand as she made her daily trek to the Century Building, her home away from home.

As she approached her office, Val was pounced on by an excited Gwen, and the day's strategy session commenced with a detailed description of the party.

"So amazing!" Gwen sank into the visitor chair next to Val's desk. "I can't believe how many people came!"

"I know," Val said, distracted. She kept recalling her awkward behavior with John and didn't want to revisit it with her cousin. She tried to steer the conversation to work, hoping in vain Gwen wouldn't bring it up.

"And you ran off!" Gwen scolded. When Val tried to explain her sudden sickness, Gwen cut her short. "John Hatfield told me he talked to you. He's single, you know," she said, deliberately goading Val. Gwen constantly teased Val about her lack of romantic interests, not that Gwen had any of her own.

"What did he say?" Once again, color rose in Val's cheeks. She hated how easily she blushed. Her lack of a poker face infuriated her.

"Your PR representative was very persuasive," Gwen said in a terrible impression of John's voice. "What in the world did you say to him?"

"I didn't say anything," Val said, "I talked to him for approximately two seconds before I left. I can't imagine why he'd even give me a second thought."

"He mentioned something about your purse." Gwen furrowed her brow as she tried to remember his exact comment. Much to Val's relief, she couldn't, and that seemed to be the end of it. With only a slight verbal nudge from Val, they moved on to campaign details.

Gwen left a few hours later. Val took a moment to look out her window and take in the beautiful day. The leaves on a few scattered trees had begun to change color and crowds of people milled about on the street below.

Val adored her office. It was a tiny piece of heaven nestled between the offices of two larger firms – an insurance company and a marketing firm called Xtra that Val sometimes worked for. As she walked by their doors, she always noted the missing "E" in their name and pondered for the millionth time how many "X" related words floated around the business world.

Val's office contained a hodgepodge of her professional life. Framed posters from charity events lined one wall. Across from her desk, a bookshelf overflowed with books from promoted authors, graphics design books, books about public relations, event planning, marketing, and a slew of other relevant business titles she almost never referred to anymore. At the back of the office, a window overlooked the street below. She had her desk positioned sideways out from the rear wall so she could lean her head up against the window and take in the bustle of life below.

Downtown Cambria was quaint yet full of modern cuisine and shopping, with musicians and street performers entertaining weekend crowds. Val spent more time gazing out the window and less time actually joining in the activity below, but she loved every second of it.

Her average day consisted of about nine to twelve hours at her desk, typing, doing research, and creating multi-media marketing materials. She enjoyed going out to meet with clients for strategic planning sessions, yet she cherished the comfort and safety of her office. Sitting amidst all the trappings of her professional life gave her a sense of purpose, made her feel like all her work compensated for the total lack of social life.

She founded Shakely PR & Marketing eight years before. After a tough start, she'd finally hit her stride. So what if she didn't even have a pet, much less a boyfriend, to keep her company at night? She had developed into a successful businesswoman, respected in the community, and that was enough.

The far corner of her office held one plant constantly on the verge of death. Val would be the first to admit she was a terrible plant owner. She found herself so wrapped up in projects the watering somehow slipped her mind. Seeing the shriveled leaves reaffirmed her decision not to get a pet. Making a mental note to toss out this latest casualty, she saved work on her current document. Time for lunch.

The interior of the Century Building housed a variety of professional offices. At street level it also hosted some amazing local shops, full of great gifts and food. Val decided to grab a sandwich at the downstairs deli.

"Hi, Jim," Val said with a smile as the insurance agent next door walked into his office.

"Hey, Val. How's your Humane Society project going?" Jim was a serious dog lover. Val didn't know much about him except he always asked about her pet-friendly projects when they ran into each other.

"Really great, actually," Val said. "The fundraiser garnered almost $40,000 for their new facility."

"Amazing! I need to hire you to work for me," Jim said, grinning. He'd made this comment to Val every time he'd seen her for the past two years but had never once talked to her about anything other than dogs. Val gave him a friendly wave and headed out the door.

Born and raised in Cambria, Val knew she'd return, even though she went away to college. The city nestled at the foot of the Rocky Mountains. It had evolved into an interesting mix of college town, hippy chic, and old, established society. Families brought to Colorado by the Gold Rush had stayed put for generations, starting industries, creating artistic and cultural institutions, and ingraining themselves so deeply into the city they sometimes found it hard to let outsiders in.

Nonetheless, the atmosphere of the town was invigorating. Val loved the charitable spirit that existed on all levels of society. She worked and lived downtown, comfortable and content with her life. She enjoyed a casual stroll over the cobblestone walkways of the shopping district and took in its energy.

When Val returned upstairs, food in hand, she sat down at her computer and started her daily reading. She perused two or three local websites that covered local business and politics. Her favorite site, Jabber, contained anonymous yet insightful posts with a critical view. The mysterious blogger prompted a good amount of speculation, given the insider information that appeared daily. Val had been both excited and scared to see what might pop up about Gwen.

Sure enough, a picture of her cousin at the previous night's party appeared with the headline "Can Gwen Marsh Win on Looks Alone?".

Val bristled. Gwen was certainly a beautiful woman, yet also bright and fully committed to her work in the community. *Why did so many people get hung up on her looks?*

The post outlined Gwen's lack of funds, her refusal to take corporate donations, and the blogger's bleak conclusion about the likely result of the campaign. Val absolutely despised the insinuation that Gwen couldn't win this election on merit alone. *Jerk*, Val thought. *The picture even makes Gwen look like more of a socialite than a serious politician.*

She closed her browser in a huff and turned to the afternoon's tasks. By the end of the day, Val completed four press releases and a flyer, posted several times on social media for Gwen's campaign, and found time to attend to the needs of her other clients. Gwen had hired Val nearly full-time, and though Val knew it devoured a huge portion of her cousin's campaign budget, she couldn't talk her out of it. So Val made sure she gave the campaign every bit of her effort and attention. Exhausted and prepared for a quiet night, Val locked up and headed downstairs.

She reached the front door, looked out, and saw none other than John headed straight for her. *Good grief, I must be cursed*, she sighed. When she opened the door, a chilly blast of air preceded the handsome gentleman.

"Ms. Shakely." He said with a nod, grinning.

Does he always look this smug?

"Mr. Hatfield. It was good to meet you last night." Val shifted about uncomfortably, not quite sure what to do. John stared silently, making her even more nervous. She couldn't take the tension and took a step toward the door. "Well, I don't want to keep you from wherever you're headed. Have a good night," she said and tried to walk past him.

"Wait, Ms. Shakely. May I speak with you for a moment?" Despite the chill, he lingered.

"Call me Val, please." She studied him for a moment, watching him gather his thoughts. "What can I do for you?"

"I wonder if you're familiar with the Hope Foundation?" He closely watched for her response.

Val raised an eyebrow. "Yes, I am. In fact, I sent you an invitation last fall for their annual fundraiser. You declined to attend, if memory serves." Val tried to assume a stern expression and was pretty certain she failed.

"Um, yes." John seemed to be gauging her reaction, studying her. "I've taken a new interest in their organization. Could you possibly tell me the best person to contact to discuss a charitable contribution?"

"I'm pretty sure it's listed on their website." *I put it there myself,* she thought. *This can't be what he wants to talk about.* "Can I do anything else for you, Mr. Hatfield?"

"No. Thank you. You've been very helpful. And please, call me John. Good night, Val." He smiled before heading into the building.

Completely perplexed, Val turned and headed home. Two interactions in two days, and each time she met this man it ended with her feeling flushed and frustrated. A consummate over-analyzer, Val took much longer walking home than usual as she pondered John and the conflicting rush of emotions that flooded her senses each time they met.

CHAPTER 2

John still smiled as he headed to his car an hour later. His mother used to call it his "Cheshire Cat" grin. Not a particularly cheerful person, John simply felt satisfied with his life, his decisions, and his actions. So he smiled. A lot.

Of course, Val probably interpreted his smile as smugness. He could tell that he bothered her, and it tickled him, even though he encountered a twinge of guilt. Not a mean person, he had nothing but respect for Val professionally, what little he knew of her anyway.

After the party, he'd taken it upon himself to research her. Reading through her website, he pondered Val's professional philosophy, trying to comprehend her based on the list of charities she supported. She seemed to be all about her career, and while the Internet was full of the evidence of her work and community involvement, he still couldn't get a clear sense of who she was as a person.

John headed into the chilly night barely aware of the walk toward his car, his mind absorbed elsewhere. *You could just ask her about herself, like a normal person would*, he admonished himself.

Of course, he probably wouldn't. Not very social himself, to simply ask Val about herself wasn't something he normally did. Why did he take such delight in making her nervous? He thought about the blush that swept across her cheeks, both at the party and then again this evening, and he found himself fascinated. What did he do that flustered her? He enjoyed getting a reaction out of Val, and he found her flushing, frazzled face alluring. His mind continued to spin, and when he pulled into his garage, he realized he'd been so lost in thoughts that he couldn't even remember the drive.

He made himself a cup of tea and looked out the window at the city below. He lived in a modestly upscale apartment in the hills overlooking Cambria. The city lights indicated a hustle and bustle that neither enticed nor comforted him. Although reclusive, he'd somehow managed to become one of the best-known men in town. How ironic. Well, maybe not so ironic.

John's father had founded Hatfield Paper Products and built it into a prosperous corporation with plants in Colorado and the Pacific Northwest. John had gone to college to get degrees in business and finance while working at his father's company. He traveled frequently to the production plant outside of Seattle. So frequently, he'd planned to take over management of that location. Then his father passed away without warning, and the fate of the company landed squarely in John's hands.

He mused about the years since his father's death. Up to that point, he'd remained in the shadows of his high-society parents, one of Cambria's power couples and regulars at all the city's most notable social events. The strained relationship with his father made John feel he never measured up to his old man's expectations, even when John's own dream was to follow in his footsteps. He loved the family business, despite his father's ambivalence toward him, and contented himself with company operations while his parents played the social circuit.

John reluctantly grabbed the social spotlight after his father died, escorting his mother to functions when his brother David was unavailable, and praying all the while those appearances came infrequently. His reputation as a recluse became the subject of endless chatter among Cambria's elite circles. He never desired to mingle and only appeared in social situations when he absolutely couldn't refuse.

His decision to attend Gwen's kick-off party confounded him. He liked the spunky young politician but saw her mayoral bid as a sinking ship. He'd never met Gwen in person until the party. He'd followed her run for city council and her ensuing years in office with something bordering on amazement. She genuinely seemed to live by her ethics and that, in John's experience, was almost unheard of.

Aware of the relationship between Val and her cousin, he knew they were quite different – Gwen an open book, Val a mystery. Val appeared in the background of some of Cambria's most prestigious and well-attended events. She supported practically every local charity, involved herself in a number of service groups, and had run a successful business for years without any discernible tension, unhappy customers, or bad reviews other than Barton's rather ridiculous squawking when she'd declined his offer to work for his campaign. John had dismissed Barton's public outrage as a childish tantrum by a spoiled politician. He furrowed his brow over the puzzle that was Val. Feeling increased tension, John rubbed his forehead and forced himself to relax.

He rarely took this great an interest in anyone, and it alarmed him, this stalker-like nature of interest in Val. After Gwen's party, he spent many hours online searching for even the smallest details about her life, and became utterly frustrated by the futility of his search. And so, in true stalker fashion, he'd planned to run into her. Luckily, Val worked in the same building as John's attorney, and he'd made a last-minute appointment in the hopes of seeing her. It had worked beautifully, even if their encounter proved awkward.

The memory made him momentarily self-conscious, a foreign sensation he wasn't terribly fond of. His faced flushed and he felt a rush of empathy for the lovely Val, whose cheeks seemed fated to be red in his presence. He decided he should focus his attention elsewhere. He found Val both captivating and confounding, and John had never held on to things that perplexed him. If he needed answers, he got them. And if he couldn't conquer something, he let it go.

He walked across the living room to his laptop, determined to work himself to sleep. It took only a few moments before his mind wandered again to Val. His fingers became frenzied, striking the keyboard with unnecessary force, so he finished his work, closed his laptop harder than he meant to, and went to bed.

* * *

John woke for the next few days feeling more and more tense. By Thursday, he started to wonder if he'd made himself sick in a feeble attempt at explaining away his mounting tension. He had a full day at work and then a cocktail party for Gwen hosted by one of his mother's friends that evening. It was another social event he'd decided uncharacteristically to attend, though he knew exactly why. He refused to give his intentions more than a passing thought. *In fact*, he rationalized, *it's perfectly reasonable for me to attend this party. I am, after all, John Hatfield.*

It was a conceited, self-absorbed thought required to get his mind refocused in a more productive direction.

Dressed in his favorite charcoal suit, John took a moment to look at himself in the mirror. Not a bad-looking man. Handsome, some might say. Not exactly thin but certainly not fat. Age and a hectic schedule had taken its toll on his frame. He didn't work out every day, but other than a few extra pounds, he was in pretty good shape.

He chose a deep blue dress shirt and a gray-blue patterned tie that made his dark blue eyes stand out even more than usual. He thought his eyes made him look stern – a trait which served him well in business negotiations. Calm and kind, he held his own in both difficult discussions and heated debates without making people despise him. He was actually well-liked and respected in the community.

Romantically, John hadn't had nearly the same luck. Most comfortable at home, he rarely placed himself in situations where he might find someone he wanted to spend more time with. John had only a handful of girlfriends in his life, mostly in college. He never devoted himself to those previous relationships. Work was his secure place, so he focused on his professional life. The business blossomed, the charities he supported flourished, and he entered an empty apartment each night without thoughts of loneliness as a confirmed bachelor.

The workday progressed without a hitch. By the time John headed to a late lunch, his life felt more in balance. He grabbed a burger from the stand near his office and walked across the street to the lakefront park to enjoy the sunny fall day. He had taken his second bite when he heard someone calling his name. He turned and saw his friend Jason Turri walk briskly across the street, his sandy blond hair ruffling in the breeze. Jason had worked for the city's finance department for years. He and John had been friends since high school and Jason became one of the few people who knew John as more than simply the town loner.

"Hey, I was headed up to your office." Jason sat next to John on the park bench and took a few deep breaths from rushing.

"How's it going?" John took another big bite out of his burger.

"An eventful day, to say the least. Election years get pretty tense but today's been especially stressful. Barton's on the warpath."

This wasn't news to John – Barton had always been considered a hothead. The fact that Jason mentioned it at all made John wary. Far from friends, John and Barton couldn't stand each other. Barton owned properties throughout the county and had large shares in several of the city's most profitable businesses, so he wasn't a force to be taken lightly. He was connected, a true member of the city's old boys' network, and when you got on his bad side, you stayed there.

"What's Roger mad about today?" John asked.

"You, actually," said Jason. "He saw the coverage of you at Gwen Marsh's party and he's pretty pissed off."

John frowned and took a breath. He'd known there would be some fallout from his unusual appearance, so it didn't surprise him. "Roger knows I won't vote for him." He shrugged and took another bite of burger.

"Yes. On the other hand, he's not terribly keen on you throwing your support behind the opposition. Especially Marsh."

"Attending a party doesn't equal supporting a candidate," John said, though he knew better. His presence wouldn't be taken as anything other than an endorsement of Barton's challenger.

"Oh, please, you know John Hatfield showing up at any event generates front-page news. Do you seriously support Marsh's campaign? Don't get me wrong, John, I think she's great. But she's a long shot."

"You know I don't get involved in politics," John stated with finality. He had never endorsed or financially supported a candidate for any office, not even President. He believed firmly that the money flowing through political campaigns led to corruption, and he cared too much about his community to ignore what he considered to be excessive and wasteful spending. "I do admire her integrity and grit though," he added.

Jason nodded and turned his attention to the water, lost in thought for several moments before changing the subject. "Do you want to get a beer after work?" Both avid college basketball fans, John and Jason attended or watched games. If John was going to be seen in public, it was usually at the arena or his favorite local pub.

"Sorry. I'm going to Mavis Bean's party for Marsh." Jason choked a little out of surprise and amusement, giving John a broad and knowing smile.

"Stirring things up, eh?" Jason's eyes twinkled with conspiratorial glee.

"Maybe," John said. "Actually, I thought you might go, too."

"Well, I can't pass up this kind of action. Not even for a game," Jason said, his interest clearly piqued. "You're a brave man, John," he warned, though he was obviously amused.

* * *

John drove up the driveway toward Mavis Bean's house. Mrs. Bean was another member of Cambria's aristocracy. The home sat on twenty acres of prime real estate a few minutes from downtown. The grounds, impeccably landscaped and enclosed by an elaborate wrought iron fence, looked more like a park than a residence. It had been in the family for generations and been carefully maintained. And since John's mother and Mavis had been girlhood friends, John had spent a great deal of time there as a child.

"Hi, Bernard. How are you this evening?" John said warmly to Bean's longtime butler. Bernard had aged, but John never forgot the man's kindness to him. Even as a child, John had been solitary. Where his siblings, David and June, had been quick to jump into social life with their mother, John had hung back. He observed. On visits to the Bean residence, Bernard was often John's favorite companion, fixing him a snack and talking about school and life.

"It's good to see you, John, although I'm surprised to see you here." Bernard raised his eyebrows slightly.

John smiled, placed his coat in Bernard's outstretched hands, and followed him further into the foyer.

"My mother pretty much demanded my appearance, so I appeared." John's explanation sounded lame in his ears, and it didn't shock him to see Bernard's quizzical look.

"Well, enjoy your evening. Your mother and Mrs. Bean are in the parlor with Ms. Marsh." Bernard turned to put away John's coat before the next guests arrived.

John walked down the hall into the parlor, a huge, elaborately decorated room off the main hallway that resembled some combination of old-fashioned sitting room and ball-room. A door on the far wall led to the library, and both rooms brimmed with Cambria's elite. This was precisely the type of event John loathed. One full of obligatory small talk and not-so-idle gossip. Despite growing up and making a life within the framework of this part of Cambrian society, John was always uncomfortable in this particular social scene. He brushed past men and women and stopped to exchange hellos and pleasantries with more than a dozen before he finally reached his mother.

Anne Hatfield and Mrs. Bean sipped wine near the fireplace in the corner of the room. The women presented a picture of elegance and sophistication, though the years had been kinder to John's mother. Both women wore dark skirted suits and pearls that had probably been handed down for generations. Bean's rounded shoulders and hunched posture made her seem feebler than her sixty-two years. In contrast, John's mother appeared youthful, strong, sturdy. A delicate but confident woman, some found Anne intimidating.

The women were having an animated conversation with the stunning Gwen. Tall and slender, her dark hair fell in waves around her shoulders. Eyes bright, Gwen looked perfectly at ease with her companions. She wore a clinging black gown, modest but modern. The dress revealed her curves, making every man in the room was aware of her presence. Every man except John.

Gwen didn't hold such attention for him. It was Val who he couldn't take his eyes off of. She stood close to her cousin, listening intently to the conversation but keeping to the periphery. Val hadn't seen John approach, but his mother had. She followed his gaze to Val, smiled broadly, and said in her loudest, most obvious voice, "Oh John! You came! Mavis said you wouldn't, but I told her you wouldn't disappoint your mother."

John approached and kissed his mother on the cheek. "Hello Mother. Mrs. Bean. Ms. Marsh. Ms. Shakely. Looks like another lively night on the campaign trail." His voice sounded strangled, and he sensed Val's eyes on him.

"Mr. Hatfield! Thank you so much for coming. I heard the mayor was a bit miffed by your attendance at my campaign kick-off." Gwen's expression gave way to amusement.

John smiled. "Please, call me John. Roger isn't one of my favorite people, and vice versa. He'll get over it." John glanced at Val and saw the color flush in her cheeks. Somehow, it made him bolder.

"Ms. Shakely, are you feeling well? It seems that every time we meet you look flushed."

He realized he'd done it again without thinking. The color in Val's cheeks burned so hot John thought people might be able to feel it halfway across the room. John's smile faltered, and he was overcome by an unfamiliar feeling of regret. He silently made a pact with himself to try not to push Val's buttons.

"Yes, thank you, John. I'm quite well," Val said. She took a deep breath as if to will the color to drain from her cheeks. "And like I said last evening, call me Val."

Gwen's ears perked up at the mention of the previous night, her eyes wide. Val hadn't mentioned running into John, and the tension in the current conversation seemed to arouse her curiosity. Anne and Mrs. Bean watched the interaction attentively, and the older women gave each other a knowing glance.

Oblivious, John added, "And you can call me John, remember?"

He took a moment to examine Val from head to toe. She wore a flattering indigo cocktail dress. Her dark hair swept up on one side to reveal the curves of her neck. Not as slender as her cousin, John found Val undeniably beautiful. There was depth in her hazel eyes and a confident air despite her incessant blushing.

Heat swept across John's own cheeks as she met his eyes. He looked away nervously. He hated feeling nervous, and in an attempt to overcome his anxiety, he struck out boldly. Wasn't the best defense a good offense?

"Val, I wonder if you'd join me for a glass of wine?"

He held out his elbow as if to lead Val but quickly took it away, aware of the familiarity of the gesture. He let his hands slide down his side where they stayed stiffly pinned, like they were held in place with iron shackles.

Val nodded and followed John hesitantly away from the small group of intrigued onlookers. It seemed like every person in the room turned to watch as they walked by. By the time they reached the bar, Val felt flustered, not used to this much attention from anyone, especially someone like John. Having him single her out this way made Val feel extremely exposed. John wiggled a finger between his tie and collar in an attempt to loosen its stranglehold. They got their glasses of wine and made their way to a quieter corner of the room.

They glanced over to where the older ladies and Gwen had resumed their conversation, joined by several other guests, among them, a very animated Jason Turri. John tried to catch Jason's eye to wave a hello, but he was too engrossed in his conversation. In fact, Jason's attention focused entirely on Gwen, and John suspected it was more than professional admiration.

"Well, how awkward," Val said. She took a large sip of wine and followed it with a big breath to calm her nerves. "I didn't expect to see you here. I've never encountered you once until a few nights ago, and now you seem to pop up everywhere."

"It has been a bit out of the ordinary for me," John said. He scanned the room, making momentary eye contact with at least a dozen people who immediately returned to their own conversations.

"So, what brings *you* here?" Val asked.

John's head snapped around in her direction. Val's hand went to her mouth, her expression a combination of shock at having spoken so rudely and earnest curiosity about his unexpected public appearances.

John bristled. "A personal invitation," he said, rather curtly, "but I don't understand why Mrs. Bean has taken such a public interest in Gwen's campaign. I can't remember her ever getting this involved in politics before."

"Maybe she's just a principled person and knows a good thing when she sees it." Val was on the defensive, fuming, agitated. In a few seconds, the evening had gone from tense and awkward to hostile. She didn't know if she liked John, and for some reason he seemed to take delight in making her angry.

"Look, I think Gwen is an excellent choice for the office, but I don't think she has a chance of winning. You can't run a campaign against Barton without money. It's that simple." John said this unemotionally, as if the truth hardly deserved mentioning.

"Gwen has beaten the odds before. Don't count her out so easily," Val countered. Their voices seemed oddly loud, and it horrified her to see a small group listening to their conversation. She shifted her body so John had to face her and then lowered her voice. "Regardless of how you feel about Gwen's campaign, please keep your voice down."

Not wanting to make more of a spectacle of himself, John shifted tactics. He didn't want to lose Val's attention. "So why are you working public relations for Gwen's campaign? From what I understand, you've never taken on a political candidate before."

"True. I've avoided politics. Too much money is spent on campaigning. But I admire Gwen's approach, so I'm supporting her." Talking about politics in general and Gwen's campaign in particular made Val feel on a level playing field with John. Well-educated and informed in these areas, she was back in her comfort zone.

"I couldn't agree more. Actually, that's what piqued my interest in her as a candidate. Are you two close?" John saw an opportunity to get some questions answered. He banked on the fact that the more he got to know Val, the less interesting she would seem. He might even be bored. The idea was a relief.

"She's my cousin, and we've always been close. Our family is spread out, but Gwen and I have always wanted to stay in Cambria. We've depended on each other. We're family." Val smiled with genuine affection as she spoke.

John studied her for a moment. "So, who are *you*, Val Shakely? I can't figure it out." It was a ridiculous question, yet it seemed the shortest way to get to what he wanted.

"Wouldn't you like to know," she said coyly and blushed at her sudden nerve. Two minutes ago they'd argued and now she flirted? What in the world did this man do to her! "Honestly, I'm just an ordinary person," she said, hoping he'd drop the subject. The lift in his eyebrows told her it hadn't served as a sufficient answer.

"I don't believe you, Val."

The color rushed back to her face, and she groaned. Clearly, Val would spend her entire evening in full blush with John around.

She shrugged. "Really, I am! In fact, I'm something of a work-aholic. I spend a lot of time on community projects. There's not that much to me. I don't even have a pet, for goodness sake!" She grimaced at her attempt to lighten the mood. It didn't work. John stared at her intently, wanting more. "You still don't look entirely satisfied with that answer," she finally said.

"Not yet," John said. "You're still a mystery." Her answers hadn't given him much to go on, and he found himself challenged. He'd hoped to get her out of his head. Instead, his curiosity continued to grow, and he was determined to know her better.

An unfamiliar knot formed in Val's stomach. She found John's handsome, brooding features absolutely intoxicating, and she transformed into a total idiot around him – even though he was an obnoxious, arrogant, entitled man. Yet, there was something fascinating and alluring about John. Val wanted to know him, too, although as soon as she thought that, a sense of terror overwhelmed her.

Not particularly lucky in love, Val had no idea what to make of this guy. John was almost a caricature of the dark brooding protagonist in her favorite romance novels. Jane Austen's Mr. Darcy combined with Emily Bronte's Heathcliff and a good dose of Charlotte Bronte's Mr. Rochester. These were the characters women usually went nuts for. Val, though she loved those books, had always stuck with men she could easily read, not dark and mysterious individuals. There was something comfortable about a nice shallow man, selfish and simple. The more she thought about her type, the more she realized her taste in men required some adjustment.

John differed from the men she usually found attractive. He made her nervous and uncertain, two of her least favorite feelings. Looking up, she realized she'd been lost in thought, and John peered at her quizzically, waiting for more.

"What exactly would you like me to tell you, Mr. Hatfield ... er, John?"

"I think I'm going to have to discover it on my own." He flashed a handsome and completely smug smile, as if she posed merely a simple hurdle to jump. She found herself feeling both irritated by him and also amused. What a strange mix!

"Well, like I said, there's not much to me, so I doubt you'll have to work very hard."

"Hmm. I very much doubt that, Val."

She loved the way her name sounded in his low, gravelly voice.

Just as she worked out something stunningly pithy to say to him, someone tapped at her shoulder. Gwen's voice whispered in her ear, "You're the center of attention." Val could hear the smile on her lips.

Val glanced around and caught two dozen sets of eyes quickly turning their attention elsewhere. Practical as always, she reminded herself this party was about creating a stir for Gwen's campaign. Guilt washed over her for having gotten so caught up in the elusive and dreadfully handsome John Hatfield.

"Excuse me, John. I'm going to mingle with the other guests," Val said abruptly.

Without waiting for a response, she walked to the opposite corner of the room, leaving John and Gwen behind. Reaching safety, Val turned and found John had disappeared. She surveyed the room but couldn't see him anywhere.

A few women she knew through her civic activities came up and started chatting busily about the party, Gwen's dress, and the campaign's next steps. Val gave her head and shoulders a small shake, forcing herself to return to the task at hand.

Small talk and handshakes made up the rest of the evening. By the time the party wound down, Val had spoken with at least a hundred people and felt positive about her work in Gwen's campaign. Support for Gwen continued to grow, and more than one person had remarked about recent press Val had generated, stroking her ego and providing a sense of accomplishment that drove her forward even under the worst of circumstances.

The last few guests still lingered close to Gwen at midnight, and since Val had come with her cousin, she sat around, rather bored, waiting for her ride home. She hadn't seen John the rest of the evening. He'd completely disappeared from the party.

Mrs. Bean had retired earlier in the night and invited Gwen and Val to make themselves at home, so Val decided to poke around the nearby rooms while she waited for Gwen. The parlor opened into a library and now, with the crowds gone, Val could actually get to the books. She perused titles and flipped through anything that looked interesting, glancing every once in a while toward the parlor where Gwen engaged in conversation.

Val was flipping through an old book on Cambria's history when she sensed someone walk up behind her. Expecting Gwen, she stifled a small shriek when she turned and found John standing so close to her she could feel his breath.

"Good grief, you scared me half to death," she said, trying to regain composure.

"I'm sorry, I've been sitting over in the corner the entire time you've been here. I thought you saw me." John smiled broadly.

Val looked past him and noticed a small sitting area. How long had he been watching her?

"I came with Gwen, so I'm keeping busy until she's ready to go."

"Doesn't look like you're going anywhere soon. Join me?" John nodded his head in the direction of the corner. Val reshelved the book and followed him to a plush couch. She sat on one end and shifted her body slightly toward John who'd taken a seat near the other end of the couch.

"I thought you'd gone home," she said nervously, making small talk.

"Were you looking for me?" A grin crept over John's lips which made his eyes twinkle.

"Um, no, well, I mean ..." Val stammered. "I just didn't see you after we finished talking, and I assumed you'd left," she said lamely.

"I escaped to the kitchen and hung out in the quiet for a while. I'm not terribly comfortable at parties." He gazed at her intently, waiting for something, though Val couldn't imagine what.

"Your mother and Mrs. Bean are friends then?" Val knew the pair often participated in community projects together, but had no idea what their relationship might be outside the public sphere.

He nodded. "Since before my birth. My siblings and I spent a great deal of time here as children. Mostly shuffled off to the kitchen or the garden while they played bridge or entertained the other society hens."

Val had begun to suspect John wasn't the snobby rich boy she and others assumed he was. He didn't seem to fit easily into Cambria's high society scene. His discomfort with people was actually endearing.

"I've seen this house about a thousand times in pictures

and driving by, but it's my first time inside. It's gorgeous." Val glanced around the room admiringly.

Cambria was her hometown, but her family didn't belong in this part of society. She was like a country mouse in the sophisticated surroundings – curious and yet intimidated, afraid to touch anything or leave any evidence of intrusion.

"Have you always lived in Cambria?" John asked in an attempt to open her up.

"Yes, except for college. I went to a university in Washington state and then came back to open my business." Val relaxed as she studied her surroundings.

"I went to an in-state college," John volunteered. "I'm the black sheep of my family. David and June, my brother and sister, attended Ivy League schools and have successful legal careers. I never wanted to do anything but run the family business.

"My father seemed both pleased and disappointed at my decision," John said, "like I'd chosen correctly but for the wrong reasons. In fact, I think that was his general feeling about me. Sometimes he was proud, and sometimes I couldn't seem to do things well enough." He grew silent, distracted.

"My father owned an office supply store in the city," Val said, emboldened by John's frankness. "I grew up working there. He inspired me. He devoted himself to the community, and he worked tirelessly on all sorts of projects and programs. I remember attending meetings and political rallies with him.

"He was kind but firm, and he could make people listen to him. I saw the belief in their eyes, buying into his dreams and causes. I have always tried to emulate him."

"Is the business still around?" John asked, surprised he hadn't seen anything in his searches.

"Uh, no. He closed the business about ten years ago and died a few years later." Val's tone reflected despair, and John borne an almost uncontrollable urge to reach out and hold her. "I think his heart broke."

"What happened to him?" John asked with genuine curiosity. He saw something in Val that she rarely revealed to the world, and he didn't want her to shut him out.

Val sighed. "Local politics. He had no interest in running for office himself, but he certainly had opinions about how to make Cambria a better place. He backed a local candidate and the opposition crushed his business. I remember talking to him every day about the situation while in grad school. He couldn't believe how personal the attacks got. Finally, he simply couldn't keep his head above water. Business dried up, and nothing he'd ever done in the community seemed to matter much anymore."

Val's sadness washed over John, a palpable and suffocating wave of anguish. She saw him take a deep breath and she followed suit before she changed the subject.

"And you, John?" she said with effort. She neared exhaustion, and the vision of her cozy bed grew more irresistible. "Why are you such a mystery? I mean, everyone knows you but no one does."

"Just a private person, I guess." He wanted to tell her more. He wanted nothing more than to have this woman know him but Gwen interrupted. She scuttled over and plopped herself down in the armchair near Val.

"Jeez! I'm so tired I could sleep right here," Gwen said with an overly dramatic sigh. Despite her feigned exhaustion, she beamed, clearly in her element. "Please tell me you're ready to go, Val." She looked up and comprehended her intrusion. "Oh, gosh, I'm sorry."

"It's okay, Gwen. I'm tired, too." She turned to John. "I enjoyed our talk. I hope it's not the last time." As bold a statement as Val could make at the late hour and following such a heavy conversation, but she meant it.

"Good night, Val. Gwen." He escorted them to the door where a tired looking Bernard met them with their coats.

Gwen cocked an eyebrow at Val once they'd settled in her

car. "Man, is he into you," she said with a hint of envy. Gwen was used to being the center of attention, the coveted one. She loved Val dearly, so the twinge of jealousy didn't linger.

"He's very different than how I imagined," Val said. She didn't go into further detail, and soon she had Gwen babbling about the party and the election. By the time Gwen dropped her off in front of her building, it was nearly two a.m. Val dragged herself upstairs, kicked off her shoes, and didn't even take her coat off before throwing herself down on the bed. She fell asleep almost before her head hit the pillow.

* * *

Across town, John settled in front of his laptop for some work, still too keyed up from the evening to think about bed, but his mind continued to wander. Visions of lovely Val and her sad eyes kept popping up in his mind. She was anything but uncomplicated and the bits of information he'd been able to gather from her made him yearn to know more. Even more unsettling, was the growing feeling of wanting to protect her, to shield her from the ugliness of the world.

He sighed heavily. He needed to get over his infatuation with Val. Too distracting. Too all-consuming. And yet, when he finally went to sleep, he smiled with thoughts of her running through his head.

CHAPTER 3

For Val, the next few days were a whirlwind of activity. With the election only three months away, Gwen's campaign manager, Victoria Dunning, scheduled appearances with a fury and negotiated with the opposition camp over the inevitable and crucial debates.

Val worked late every night to squeeze in other client projects and to pump out marketing materials and press releases at a pace she knew she couldn't maintain forever. A little self-pity, moaning, and groaning about her workload and the stress of the campaign seeped through. Nevertheless, every morning Gwen popped into her office, coffee in hand, and the work flowed. As much as she hated to admit it, Val enjoyed herself more often than not.

She surfed the web each morning, and other than the cynical remarks about Gwen that appeared every few days on Jabber, the overall reception of her cousin was favorable. She was behind in the polls, but her numbers had improved. Overwhelmingly, she was the more likable candidate. Of course, Barton made that easy. He'd already launched personal attacks on Gwen, noting her lack of experience and her youth, labeling her as nothing but a pretty party girl who had no business sitting in a seat as important as that of Mayor. He stopped short of implying that women as a group weren't fit for the role, and he received some major flak for his attacks, especially from women's groups in town.

Friday finally arrived, and Val was in need of some relaxation. Around midday, she pressed her face against the office window, staring down at the shoppers passing by. She noticed a well-dressed man holding a sign. He wore a hat and she couldn't see his face. As he tilted the sign in her direction, she saw the words "Have lunch with me Val" written in huge bubble-shaped script.

She laughed out loud and, as if the sign-holder sensed it, he looked up. Her gaze locked onto John's dark eyes. Despite her hectic schedule and general avoidance of romantic entanglements, her heart fluttered as she focused on his ridiculous grin. After their talk at Mrs. Bean's, Val had spent a great deal of time thinking about him, and the chance to spend more moments with him thrilled her.

Not waiting to talk herself out of it, Val grabbed her coat, wrapped her scarf around her neck, pulled her dark hair out from its folds, and headed downstairs. By the time she reached the front door, Val almost convinced herself she'd imagined the whole thing. Then she walked out to meet him.

"Hi." John rolled up his poster and shoved it in a nearby trashcan, clearly embarrassed by his own romantic antics.

"Hi back." Val smiled up at him. For the first time, she noticed how tall he was.

"Where do you like to eat around here?" he asked, assuming quite correctly that his bid for a lunch date had succeeded.

"There's a great deli around the corner," she said, and off they went.

Over lunch they chatted about their lives – jobs they'd had, favorite college classes, their families. Val and her older sister, Liz, hadn't been close since their dad died. Her mom lived near Liz and provided updates on the goings on in the rest of the Shakely family, though their conversations often seemed forced. Besides Gwen, Val had no relatives living close by and, honestly, she only rarely missed them.

Her father's death had rocked the foundation of Val's family. She and her mother had been at odds over her father, because her mom had a hard time understanding his depression after losing his business. As a tough and resilient woman, she expected him to bounce back. When he didn't, their marriage suffered.

Her mother had relied heavily on Liz during this period. The rift between Val and her mother had been gentle compared to the abyss that seemed to open between Val and her sister. They'd never found their way back to one another.

Val loved her mother, but their relationship seemed to work better living halfway across the country from each other, too far away for frequent visits. Val enjoyed her solitude. She had worked extremely hard to get her business going. Now, with a steady clientele, there was a sense of comfort in her life. The solitude was like a badge of honor that provided Val with the confidence she didn't need anyone else, even when she knew it wasn't entirely true.

John talked enthusiastically about his company, and Val realized how much he loved it. He described his siblings' legal careers – his sister a successful attorney in upstate New York and his brother running, unopposed, for his third term as a Colorado Court of Appeals judge, on the fast track toward a federal judicial appointment. John mentioned he and his brother were close but rarely saw one another despite living in the same city. They took turns escorting their mother to social events, but it seemed John took the lion's share these days.

The conversation grew lively and intense. Both highly opinionated, they tended to throw each other off-kilter enough to find contention on even the most innocuous of topics. When they landed on the subject of the campaign, Val finally lost her cool.

"I don't understand why you're so relentlessly negative about Gwen's campaign," she finally exclaimed, exasperated. "She's young, yes, but she's got passion. The old boys political crap is absolutely ridiculous!"

Val's temperature rose. John's matter-of-fact dismissal of Gwen made her blood boil. In fact, her heightened emotions made his calmness especially aggravating.

John shrugged. "Hey, it's not that I dislike Gwen, I just think she's fighting an uphill battle. Barton is a shark, and he's already giving her a beating in the media." Val wasn't the only one getting irritated. Her blow-up had finally rattled John, and he vented his frustration with her defensiveness, especially in terms of an election where he believed his opinion reflected a reality Val didn't seem willing to face. "I know this town, that's all."

"So, you don't think things can change? That's a pretty bleak view of the city you claim to love." Val couldn't fathom why she was so upset and defensive with John. Only a few moments ago, when she'd seen him standing on the street with his sign, Val practically rushed out to meet him, and now she argued with him like he was her enemy.

John took a moment to consider Val. When she got defensive, she proved to be passionate, intelligent, and stubborn. At times, he wanted to wrap his arms around her and hold her tight. Then came moments like this one where he wished he'd stayed at his office.

"Look, Val, I know I'm not the easiest person to get along with. That doesn't mean what I'm saying isn't true." He sighed and said, in the best conciliatory tone he could muster, "It's also not intended to bash Gwen. She's an excellent councilwoman, and if it were up to me, I'd elect her over Barton in a heartbeat."

Val willed herself to calm down. Now she hated how ridiculous she turned around John. He made her feel irrational without much effort. Actually, Val's tendency to overreact and especially her propensity for blushing constantly was one of her least favorite traits. Quick to anger, Val had to admit she held onto grudges far too long. John's mere presence made her look deeply at herself, and what she saw wasn't flattering.

They walked back to the Century Building in silence – John brooded and Val agonized. When they reached the door of her building, Val's mind was made up to take things back to a professional level. She turned around to say goodbye and was surprised to find John smiling widely, conspiratorially. Once again, he'd caught her off-guard. Before she could say a word, he leaned down, kissed her lightly on the cheek, and walked away.

For a few moments, Val stood, mouth agape, completely unable to move. Her cheek burned where John's lips had brushed against it. The sensation startled her so much, she almost lifted her hand to touch the affected area. *John Hatfield, what in the world are you doing to me*, she thought and headed upstairs to finish her day.

* * *

Standing outside Val's building, John had sensed her tension and experienced overwhelming compassion. It occurred to him quite often these days that any woman who spent time with him had her work cut out. Val challenged him, openly and passionately. He didn't know if he liked it, but he knew he couldn't let her walk away from him – he could sense a brush off in the making. So he did the most impulsive thing he'd ever done. He kissed her and then retreated before she had time to slap him – if women did that anymore.

He didn't know what to make of the strange effect Val had on him. He'd never wanted to be with someone so badly, but she frustrated him, left him feeling unsettled. She was guarded, hard to read, reluctant to open up. He loved to hear her talk about her work, how clearly she cherished what she did. Val had a solid reputation in the city and had earned a loyal following. From her passion on numerous topics, he understood why. Yet, she hesitated to delve into her feelings about family, her father in particular. John realized how hard this loss continued to be for her. Plus, she was so damned defensive about Gwen. How could a person in public relations be so unrealistic about her client?

Okay, John thought, *so maybe it was unfair to expect her to be completely rational about her cousin.* Client or no, Val hadn't taken the job based on money. She certainly believed in her cousin as a viable candidate. John made a mental note to take it easy on the topic of Gwen's campaign in conversation, if possible.

John reached his office and stepped into the middle of an uproar. Barton waited for him while John's secretary, Iris, paced furiously in front of the office door. Barton had bullied his way past her and prepared to pounce the second John walked in.

John reassured Iris and readied himself for the onslaught. Sucking in one last deep breath, he opened his office door and walked through.

"Mayor," John said formally and without a hint of friendliness. He barely hid his irritation at the intrusion, intentionally avoiding eye contact with Barton in hopes the politician would get the hint he was not welcome.

"Dammit, John! What in the hell are you thinking giving your support to little Gwennie Marsh?" Barton practically spat the name. His face had turned an ugly purplish-red.

"Ms. Marsh is an excellent candidate, Roger. I'd appreciate if you wouldn't disparage her in my office. Especially since you're here uninvited." John was determined to keep his cool despite Barton's antagonism.

"Look, John. I know you don't like me, but you need to stay out of this."

John heard the threat, clumsily concealed in the warning statement. Barton studied him, waiting for a reaction.

"Roger, I'll support whomever I damned well please." His anger rose, and he looked at Barton dismissively. "I'm sure you can find the door on your own." John turned his back and fiddled with some random papers on his desk until he heard the politician stand up and take a few steps toward the door. Then Barton paused and turned again in John's direction.

"Understand this, John. If you continue to lend support to Ms. Marsh, you'll regret it." And the door closed with a thud.

John took a seat behind his desk and fumed. Why the hell did Barton's feel so threatened by Gwen? There was an air of desperation in the threat. Did Gwen stand a better chance of winning than he'd thought?

Whatever the reason, Barton's behavior was unusually hostile and angry. John believed he had meant to be physically intimidating, and if he hadn't had several inches on Barton, it might have worked. John made a mental note to steer clear of the mayor when possible and then got started on his own work.

CHAPTER 4

After dark, Val made her way out of the office for the chilly and short walk home. Exhausted, she looked forward to sleeping late the next morning. About two blocks from her apartment, Gwen's car passed her then stopped. She parked, hopped out, walked Val the rest of the way, followed her into the apartment, and threw herself on the couch in a rather theatrical fashion.

"What a week!" Gwen happily accepted the cup of tea Val passed her a few moments later. "What's on the agenda for tonight?"

Val groaned. Hanging out on Friday nights with Gwen was a normal part of their lives, but tonight Val wanted to go to bed with a book. She'd been around so many people all week that she craved some alone-time. "Gwen, I'm tired. Can we maybe do this tomorrow night?"

"Um, no. Tomorrow night we're heading over to Governor Carlton's house for a dinner party." Gwen sipped her tea and looked for the remote.

"Ugh. I forgot. Do I really need to attend every event with you, Gwen?" Val hoped her cousin might sense her need for some downtime and take pity on her. No such luck.

"You *have* to come, Val. Besides, John will be there," Gwen said in a conspiratorial tone.

"Hmm. He didn't mention it at lunch today," Val said and smiled, amused at her cousin's raised eyebrows.

She thought for a moment about telling Gwen the whole story, ultimately deciding to stick to the highlights. She kept the kiss to herself, though she could feel her cheeks warm as she thought about it.

"I don't get why he's showing such interest in your campaign," Val added, after recounting the lunch date.

Gwen feigned a pout. "Possibly because I'm an amazing candidate." Seeing the alarmed look on Val's face, Gwen giggled. "Honestly Val, he couldn't care less about my campaign. That's not why he shows up." She winked.

Val sputtered her sip of tea. "Oh, please, Gwen, we've known each other for about two minutes." The exaggeration made Val feel extremely ridiculous and curious why she tried so hard to downplay her interactions with John, especially with her cousin.

"Then why the lunch date? And the sign! Good grief, Val, he probably felt like a complete idiot standing outside your window hoping you'd see him. It's got to be love."

Despite her best efforts, Val grinned so hard her cheeks ached. Their conversation turned toward high school antics. Gwen and Val revisited their teenage days, giggling and carrying on.

When Gwen hit the bottom of her tea cup, she stood up and said, "Fine, tired girl, I'm leaving now. I'll be back tomorrow evening at five to pick you up. You *are* going with me!"

Resigned to her fate, Val gave her cousin a hug, locked the door behind her, and headed to bed.

* * *

Despite her best intentions to sleep in, Val awoke at seven. She waged a silent protest by pulling the covers over her head and pretended to sleep, but she bored quickly with the attempt. She decided instead to grab a nap later that afternoon instead.

Item one on her agenda, a cup of coffee. No, two cups of coffee. By the end of the second cup, Val was prepared to get started with her day. She pulled on jeans and her favorite sweatshirt, a beat-up gray mess with fraying edges and the emblem of her alma mater nearly completely faded with wear. Val "borrowed" the sweatshirt from her college roommate almost fifteen years ago, and even then she knew she'd never part with it. It was soft and comfortable, a complete reflection of her current life despite the recent hustle and bustle. She slipped on her sneakers, grabbed her purse, and headed downstairs.

Fallen leaves covered her car. She pulled her arm up inside a sleeve and made big swooshing movements to clear the windshield. Then she climbed in and headed toward the mall, the rest of her car materializing out of a swirl of flying leaves. If she needed to attend more events with Gwen, she needed a slightly larger selection of dresses.

Three hours later, Val lugged her purchases across the mall's parking lot and sank onto the front seat of her car, exhausted but satisfied. Always practical, Val found an armload of dress slacks, skirts, and blouses that made an excellent campaign wardrobe. Her prize purchase was a stunning blue cocktail dress for the governor's dinner. The dress cost more than she'd ever spent on a single piece of clothing, so at first she'd tried to talk herself out of it. Finally, she swiped her credit card and resolved to skip a few breakfast burritos and mochas in the next week or two to make up for her splurge.

When she deposited her bags inside the door of her apartment, she set the alarm on her phone and napped. Her sleep was restless, and when the alarm went off, she decided that fifteen more minutes wouldn't hurt. Even then she felt tired. Alas, duty called. The hour approached four, and she needed every minute of the next sixty minutes to prepare.

Val considered herself pretty ordinary, neither slender nor fat, but something of an in-between average. Her hair, Val's most striking feature, always managed to look like she'd just stepped out of the salon without much work. It was dark brown and fell slightly below her shoulders, shiny and silky with a rolling natural wave.

She took a shower and enjoyed its steam. Then, she used the last of her "date night" body butter. By the time she started pulling on clothes and putting on makeup, Val felt pretty amazing.

Her cocktail dress was a vibrant royal blue, and its high waist and princess neckline drew attention to her usually unremarkable, but tonight completely noticeable, bust. She went the extra mile and picked out a dazzling new necklace that matched the dress. And as a finishing touch, she pulled out the only-worn-once-before Michael Kors heels that she knew made her legs look stunning.

When she opened the door for Gwen, she was pleased by the look of total shock that briefly crossed her cousin's face. Gwen wore an elegant, black floor-length dress, her hair swept up like something out of old Hollywood, and she looked sophisticated. Regardless, Val was *the* knockout tonight.

"Wow, you look amazing!" Gwen said.

The dazzling royal blue color of Val's dress made the green flecks in her hazel eyes sparkle.

Val chuckled. "You make it sound like I never dress up," she teased, knowing the chances of catching her in a dress, let alone something like the number she currently sported, was damned near miraculous.

Grabbing her black dress coat, Val took one last look in the mirror before taking Gwen's arm and setting out for the party.

* * *

Governor Rex Carlton currently served his second term in office, and he and his wife, Constance, were known to throw lavish parties in the Governor's Mansion. Val and Constance served together on Cambria's Community Foundation's board of directors, so Val was actually a returning guest to the mansion. Constance greeted her at the door with a friendly hug and then turned all of her attention to Gwen. Both candidates were scheduled to attend tonight's party, but it was no secret which one Constance favored.

Constance led the two women into the parlor for drinks and introduced them to other guests – two state senators and their spouses as well as a University of Colorado regent and her son. Barton and his wife, Kathy, arrived a few minutes later and exchanged pleasantries with the other guests. When he reached Gwen, Barton's smile took on more of a sneer as he said, rather dismissively, "Ms. Marsh." He nodded his head in acknowledgement but didn't offer his hand. His eyes swept over Val, but she said nothing.

Gwen produced her most charming smile. "It's so nice to see you, Mayor, Mrs. Barton. You know my cousin, Val Shakely? She's running public relations for my campaign."

Leave it to Gwen. Val wilted under the mayor's sudden glare.

"Yes, of course, Ms. Shakely. Funny, I thought you didn't take on political candidates as clients." Barton smiled and continued, "I guess we break a lot rules for family, eh?"

Val bristled and would have responded but a voice from behind her loudly said, "Good grief, Roger, are political candidates always so rude when invited to the Governor's Mansion?"

Val turned and saw John, his smile charming, his eyes fierce as he glowered at Barton.

A hush fell over the room. The governor strode up swiftly to break the tension. "Roger! How nice of you and Kathy to join us. Come meet Suzanne Reynolds. She's CU's newest regent." The Bartons were led off across the room.

"How that man survives in politics, I'll never know!" Gwen cried. "He's an absolute terror."

"Let's get a drink," said Constance. She seemed startled and had a strange look on her face. She took Gwen's arm and led her away to the bar leaving Val and John alone.

John's face relaxed and he smiled at Val, looking her up and down, drinking her in. "You look so beautiful tonight." He ran a hand through his hair, feeling extremely self-conscious.

Val blushed, "Thank you. You look beautiful too. I mean ..."

She snapped her jaw shut, aware of how ridiculous her comment sounded, and willed no more silliness to escape from her lips.

"Looks like tonight's going to be interesting," John chuckled half-heartedly, letting his eyes dart to where Barton now chatted casually with the senators. "I wonder if Roger can get through a whole night without turning into an asshole."

"Too late, I think," Val joked. She welcomed John as an ally when it came to Barton. She found his blatant hostility, especially in the present situation, rather disturbing.

"Would you like a drink?" John asked and offered Val his arm. She slipped her hand through, and they walked together to the bar. John ordered them each a glass of wine and, before long, dinner was announced.

The guests made their way into the formal dining room. Val found herself seated between Gwen and the regent's son. John had been placed beside the governor. Barton and his wife sat on the far end of the table, wedged between the senators who talked animatedly across from them. Dinner conversation commenced. Val thought the exquisite food lightened the mood and led to a largely pleasant evening.

The regent's son, Alfred, a talented and fairly well-known local photographer, provided a stream of amusing stories about his travels. Val had seen his work, and they conversed enthusiastically. He appeared taken with Val, and she found it difficult to glance across the table at John without feeling terribly conspicuous and rude.

After dinner, the crowd retired to the parlor, and the politicians engaged in what could only be described as a battle of wits. Barton kept his words and tone only marginally inside the bounds of politeness, not wanting to offend his hosts but barely managing to keep himself contained. Gwen held her own. She enjoyed the chance to spar with Barton on neutral ground. She also discussed politics in general with the state senators. Gwen's enthusiasm was palpable, and despite Barton's increasingly annoyed looks as the evening progressed, the senators seemed more engaged by Gwen than ever.

The party ended around eleven, and guests said their goodbyes, including the Bartons, thankfully among the first to leave. John and Val spent almost no time together the whole night. Whenever Val looked up from conversation with the energetic Alfred, she met John's gaze. She was aware of him in a very physical way, her body charged with electricity at the nearness of him.

Of course, Alfred seemed to pick up on her energy but, in his romantic vigor, he misinterpreted it as an interest in himself. Val, always wanting to avoid conflict, endured him much longer than she'd wanted to and was relieved when Alfred's mother beckoned him to leave. John, who'd been chatting with the regent nearby, walked her to her car, so he disappeared from the room as Gwen found Val.

Gwen was out of breath, eyes bright with excitement. "The governor's going to endorse my campaign!" she nearly squealed. While not exactly a shock, having the endorsement of a highly esteemed, sitting governor certainly would have an impact on Gwen's numbers.

"How wonderful, Gwen!" Val said, distractedly. She watched the front door, waiting for John to rematerialize, but he didn't.

"I'm exhausted, Val. Let me say goodbye to Constance and then let's get out of here," said Gwen, oblivious to Val's demeanor.

Reluctantly, Val followed her cousin to say goodbye to Governor and Mrs. Carlton. They gathered their coats and headed to Gwen's car. Disappointment flooded through Val and threatened to drown her. She'd spent the whole night thinking about John. Having been cornered by Alfred, she became rather disgruntled.

Val didn't spend much time or energy on romance. She barely flirted, and while it was good to have someone find her attractive, she would hardly lose sleep without it. John's entrance into her life made her feel things she'd never did before, and she didn't know if she liked it. She should be reeling from an exciting evening, but instead pouted because the handsome recluse had disappeared.

They drove home in a thick silence. Gwen, caught up in her reverie, finally said, "I hope you didn't have a terrible time. It looked like you had an admirer." She grinned.

"It was fine. Seems like you won some important support," she said, hoping to turn Gwen onto a different topic. It worked like a charm, and for the final few minutes of the drive, Gwen bubbled over with a recap of the night's conversations, Barton's barely contained hostility, and the governor's pending endorsement.

As she pulled up in front of Val's building, she said, "Oh, my gosh, Val, I could actually win," as if the thought had just occurred to her.

Val opened the car door and turned to her cousin. "Of course you can, Gwen. I have total faith. Love you." She stepped into the night, closing the door quickly to cut off any further conversation.

* * *

Val wanted to do nothing more than sink into bed and stay there for the rest of the weekend. First, she hung her stunning but completely pointless dress and pulled on her comfiest pajamas. Making one last trip to the living room, she locked the front door, dug her phone out of her bag, and padded down the hallway to her bedroom.

She sat down in bed, opened her book, and noticed her phone's flashing message light. She had forgotten she'd turned the ringer off during the party. There were several new messages. Two from her mom reminding her of their monthly chat scheduled for the next day. The last two from Gwen, a few forgotten highlights from the night and an exuberant *"See you Monday!!!!!"* She cleared the messages, sent replies, and the phone buzzed again. *Jeez, Gwen. Can't it wait?* With a deep sigh, she turned the phone over in her palm.

The text came from an unknown number. She opened the message and read, *I couldn't take my eyes off of you.*

Her mouth went completely dry and her cheeks burned with a familiar fire. She texted back. *You disappeared.*

She stared at the phone, willing it to buzz again. Two minutes. Five minutes. Her heart raced, and she got up to get a glass of water, hoping to calm her nerves. When she got back to the bedroom, she nearly dove for the phone as it buzzed on her bed.

What are you doing tomorrow? Can we meet for coffee?

Yes. Where?

Java Lite at 96th?

OK. When?

10?

Sure.

Nervousness took over – Val wasn't sure what to say next. Maybe nothing. Her phone stayed silent for another five minutes, and she started to read again, not that concentration was likely. When the phone buzzed once more. She picked it up and opened the message.

It was Gwen. *You should call that photographer.*

With a groan, Val silenced the ringer, put her phone down with a thud on the bedside table, and went to sleep.

CHAPTER 5

The sun peeked through Val's bedroom windows around six forty-five, and no matter what she did, she couldn't fall back asleep. *It's going to be another long day*, she thought, stumbling out of bed and putting on a pot of coffee.

Sunday morning was the only time Val gave herself a break from structure. She sipped coffee and scanned the TV channels until she found the local news. There was some coverage on the previous night's dinner at the Governor's Mansion. She hadn't been aware anyone had taken photos, but now it occurred to her that Alfred had his camera with him.

To her horror, she featured prominently in about half of the photos in the slideshow the anchors narrated. The male anchor noted, "… and mayoral candidate Gwen Marsh's date for the night was her cousin and campaign public relations consultant, Val Shakely. It looks like Ms. Shakely caught the photographer's eye."

Val cringed, put her mug down on the coffee table, and flopped down on the couch with a moan.

The coverage continued. "On a related note, our favorite political blogger at Jabber had a lot to say about the candidates' dinner as well."

Val shot up on the couch. Jabber had been diligently commenting on the campaign thus far, taking pot shots at both candidates with equal amounts of venom. When the blogger didn't call

Gwen out on her looks or lack of experience, he attacked her idealistic vision of politics, calling it unsustainable and suspect. And, of course, Barton's boorish and aggressive attacks made him an easy target for criticism.

The blogger's constant narrative about Gwen's appearance made Val think "he" must be a man. Now that she thought about it, not too many guests attended the governor's party. Could it be a coincidence that Alfred's photos showed up on the news alongside a segment of the blog?

Val picked up her mug and took another gulp of coffee. Now fully alert, her mind sifted through the details of the previous evening. Predictably, her thoughts kept coming back to John, and she grew quite apprehensive about their coffee date. At times, she felt about as ridiculous as she ever had as a teenager, crushing on the cute boy in class. Being around John made her feel alive like she never had before.

Val had dated infrequently, finding herself bored and unwilling to get too personal with anyone. Her two attempts at serious romances became total disasters. Her first serious boyfriend was Jacob, and the relationship had lasted about five months before she finally admitted to herself that he wasn't the one.

Jacob hadn't been supportive of Val's career. She'd been back in Cambria for about two years and had begun to feel established. Younger than her, Jacob had been covetous of her time. He found her long and unpredictable schedule annoying. When he finally told her he wanted more of her time, she dumped him. He was heartbroken and despite her love for him, she was relieved.

Since her father's death, Val had devoted herself to constructing impenetrable walls around her heart, and in the wake of the breakup with Jacob they served her well. He made several attempts to win her back, but by the time it was finally completely over, he was convinced Val never loved him. The last time they'd spoken, he'd called her cold, and that had hurt Val more than the actual breakup.

Val threw herself into her work, as she always did, and was surprised when a casual date with a new friend, Rich, turned into almost two years together. She would have married Rich. He had been her best friend, and she found herself much more willing to take time away from work to be with him.

Rich was adventurous and uninhibited. He brought Val out of herself and she liked the person she was when with him. Rich didn't want to get married. In fact, every few months he'd disappear for a several days and Val was never sure where he went.

When he resurfaced, he was always aloof, and Val went out of her way to give him space but also be available for him to rebuild their intimacy block by block.

After the third or fourth time, Val started to see Rich's disappearing act as his way of putting distance between them. Val resented his unwillingness to commit. A few weeks before their second anniversary, Val was done. Their lingering dead-end relationship had taken its toll on her whole perspective on intimacy and love. Rich called her on a Saturday morning to see if she wanted to go hiking, and she told him she needed some time off. She never heard from him again.

Ending her connection with Rich had been devastating. She didn't miss the relationship as much as she missed the person she became when she let down her walls and lived in the moment. And Val hated Rich for having been the one to draw her out. The way she saw it, before Rich, she'd been content. Life wasn't exactly exciting but it was calm, predictable.

Rich came into her life like a tornado, leaving damage in his wake. She felt and experienced more with him than she ever had, but when things were bad, she wanted to hide, crawl under the covers and never come out. She bent and molded herself to fit what she thought Rich wanted, and it was never enough. By the end, Val had begun to doubt whether she deserved love. That was her breaking point. She decided she would never allow a relationship to shake up her sense of self.

Like many good intentions, Val's determination to preserve her self-confidence didn't prove easy. Instead, she took the easy path and shut herself away from the world of dating. In truth, real love petrified her.

Val figured it stemmed back to her father. A daddy's girl and his perpetual shadow from the time she was small, Val became intrigued by him, from his business suits to the way he spoke about the world. As she grew older, her admiration also grew. She looked forward to coming home from school to tell him about her day. Her choice in colleges and fields of study were inspired by her father's work. He may have run an office supply store, but it was his passion for the local community that Val embraced in her professional goals. So much so, that she majored in business and community development.

Halfway through her graduate degree, things started to go badly for her father. Each time they talked, Val heard the strain creep into his voice until he finally confessed that the business was failing. One of his good friends had run for a position on the city council and Val's father had lent his full support. His friend's opponent, a powerful local businessman, incited a boycott on the businesses associated with the friend's campaign. Her father's business fell so fast it broke him. He'd given so much of himself to the community, yet, when he needed support, it didn't emerge.

A few months before she graduated, her father closed his business for good. His all-consuming depression created a divide between her parents. Val earned her Master's and returned home to start her own business. Having Val home cheered her father up some, but not enough. His health declined and Val watched, horrified, as her strong, charismatic father wasted away. He died two years later, and Val believed it was due to his broken heart.

Since then, Val had been guarded, both personally and professionally. In her business, she carefully chose her clients and their supported causes. She cared about her community but wouldn't involve herself in anything too controversial. She admitted it was hard to make a name for yourself when unwilling to put yourself out there. To compensate, she redoubled her efforts, worked long hours, and eventually found a comfortable, successful stride. In her personal life, she chose safety. Except for Rich and Jacob, she made a conscious decision not to get involved. She nitpicked. She invented trivial reasons to make herself unavailable. And the few men she dated fell away like leaves.

It wasn't only romantic entanglements Val avoided. She was friendly with everyone but friends with few. Conversations with her mom and sister were shallow. She loved them but couldn't quite forgive them for abandoning her father in his weakest moment. Her mom had moved to be with her sister less than six months after her dad passed, increasing Val's feeling of abandonment. Luckily, Gwen was as close to Val as a sister, and it was her cousin's persistence that solidified their relationship. Gwen knew Val's moods but didn't allow Val to push her away. And Val was grateful because she needed Gwen.

Val's coffee had gotten cold as she sat, recollecting. She took a peek at her phone – 9:09. She had to leave to meet John in about half an hour, so she got out of her head and into the shower. The hot water felt amazing. It relaxed Val and washed away the suffocating gloom which enveloped her whenever she thought of her father. Out of the shower, she threw her hair into a messy ponytail, pulled on jeans and a sweater, and headed out the door.

* * *

Val happily inhaled Java Lite's strong scent of coffee beans and spices. She saw John tucked into a cozy corner near the back of the shop. She walked up to the counter and ordered a dark chocolate mocha before she headed over to John. He stood up to greet her, and the smile that swept across his face made her heart leap a little.

Oh, this is going to be trouble, she thought as she sat down in a big plush armchair, her heart racing.

"Hi," he said, shifting his body to face her more directly. He wore jeans and a dark long-sleeved shirt under his black coat. His eyes brightened as he gazed at her. Val studied him for a moment, taking in his features and thinking, not for the first time, how deliciously handsome he was.

"Hi back. Hope you didn't have to wait too long," she said, taking a sip of her steaming drink. She'd had way too much coffee already this morning, so she tried to sip gingerly.

"Did you see yourself on the news this morning?" John asked, winking a bit.

"Yes, it was horrible," she chuckled, blushing. Val's initial feeling of having wasted her new dress on a dud of an evening diminished once she realized she had been the focus of so much attention. Luckily, she had looked amazing.

John smiled, "You were beautiful. I was a little jealous of the photographer for taking up so much of your time, though I appreciated the photographic evidence of his … er … adoration this morning." He looked positively mischievous, and she sucked in some air, more conspicuously than intended. "I didn't mean to embarrass you," he chimed in, seeing her discomfort.

"I'm not used to being in the spotlight," Val explained, lamely. She was still thinking about John thinking about her.

"Barton certainly lacked his usual charm last night," John mused. "He's often hard to deal with, but he seems to be coming unhinged. I've never known Roger to be that rude in front of so many important people. Even in the last election, he generally behaved well at public functions. Though it's hard to imagine, I think he's actually intimidated by Gwen."

"Really?" Val said, abashed. Barton *had* seemed more defensive than usual at the party, and he and his wife had left awfully early. That didn't mean he was intimidated by Gwen, did it? After all, he still led in the polls by a good margin.

"I'm beginning to rethink my stance on your cousin's campaign," John said. He studied Val's reaction and wondered what she thought. She seemed distracted.

"The party last night was certainly interesting," Val said, giving nothing away.

"You had quite the admirer," John noted. "I had the urge to lock him in a closet somewhere." John's tone seemed playful, but Val could see a spark of real irritation in his eyes.

Val chuckled. "He was a pest, but a charming one," she said kindly. John's not-so-subtle flirting flustered her. It made her nervous but also strangely bold, and she added coyly, "I kept wishing he were someone else."

John raised his eyebrows. "Oh?"

Val cleared her throat nervously and looked out the window, away from John. Her cheeks burned as they usually did in his presence, but other emotions distracted her from feeling embarrassed. Still facing away, she said, "And then you were gone ..." Last night's disappointment washed over her and she sighed.

Feeling a warm hand on her shoulder, she turned to face John. He had leaned in closer, and though her instinct prompted her to move away a bit, create some space, she held her ground. Her heart raced, and as much as she'd daydreamed about this man, the closeness overwhelmed her senses.

John's cheek brushed against hers as he said, quietly in her ear, "I couldn't take my eyes off you." The sound of his voice was electric, sending shivers and warmth through her body. She inhaled deeply and closed her eyes, savoring the feel of his skin against hers, the warmth of his face, his hair brushing against her cheek. It lasted for only a second or two, but it seemed like time had stopped. For that one moment, Val's whole body responded to his. And then, he leaned back in his seat and the moment passed.

They drank in the silence for a few minutes before the conversation went back to idle chit-chat. Afterwards, Val couldn't even remember what they'd talked about in those last minutes. The weather? Business? It was a blur. He walked Val to her car and kissed her lightly on the cheek before walking down the street in the other direction. She watched him go, torn, wanting to go after him, to be near him again, but also wanting to dash home to safety. Instead, she stood next to her car, unmoving, watching him get into his car a block down the street and merge into traffic. She waited until she couldn't see him anymore before heading home.

CHAPTER 6

On Monday morning, John noticed that he hummed as he shaved. After coffee with Val, he'd had lunch with his mother and then spent the afternoon reading and relaxing. He felt rejuvenated, alive, happier than he'd been in ages.

When he walked into his office building, he met with a wall of tension, no one quite willing to make eye contact, none of the casual atmosphere that usually greeted him. Something was up. He headed down the hall to his office, his jaw clenched in anticipation. Iris stood as he approached her desk.

"Bob Johnson called this morning," Iris said. "They're pulling their contract."

Johnson's company was one of Hatfield Paper's oldest and most reliable clients. The two companies had done business for nearly two decades.

Pushing a wave of panic aside, John's mind went into problem-solving mode. "What did he say, exactly?"

"They've decided to go in a different direction. He was very vague," said Iris. Her face registered concern.

"Get him on the phone for me."

She nodded, and John walked past her to sit at his desk. He'd logged onto his computer when the phone rang.

"Hey, Bob! How are you?" John's tone sounded forced. He needed to calm down.

"Hi, John. What can I do for you?" Johnson's voice seemed

distant, almost cold. John couldn't remember a time when they'd ever spoken with such formality.

"Well, I got in and heard you've pulled your account with us." He paused for effect. "We've worked together for years, Bob, since my father's tenure. What's going on?"

John heard a sigh. "We're simply looking at new options, John. Your company has been wonderful for us, but we're moving in a new direction."

A lump formed in John's stomach as he considered the more sinister reasons for this shift in course.

"There must be something I can do to change your mind," John said, though at this point Johnson had given him nothing to work with. "If cost is an issue, I'm sure we can work with …"

"No, that's not the problem, John. You've always been reasonable with us." He hesitated. "Look, there's nothing that can be done. We're trying something different." The tension in Johnson's voice was palpable but John persisted, hoping to at least bring the real reasons for the failing relationship to the table.

John talked with Johnson for nearly an hour, unable to change his mind or even get a direct answer about the sudden decision. When he hung up, John felt agitated. Johnson had been totally unwilling to elaborate on the detail and equally unmoved by John's appeals. To John, a person who could negotiate even the most difficult agreements, being thwarted was an uncomfortable feeling, and he hated it. He suspected Barton's recent visit to his office had something to do with the morning's tension.

John called an emergency meeting with his senior staff and, after several hours, they'd worked out a strategy for moving forward without the Johnson account. Although an unfortunate loss, it wouldn't seriously impact the business.

John met his friend Jason at The Pub for lunch. When he walked in, he found Jason sitting at a table in the corner looking harried.

"Hey, everything okay?" John asked, taking a seat and ordering an iced tea.

"It's been an incredibly stressful day. Look, I'm not sure how much credence to put into this, but I heard a pretty awful rumor this morning and I think you need to know."

"Sure," John said, hesitantly. Jason was an easy-going person, and John had never seen him spooked quite like this. It added to his already tense mood.

"Ed Hillory at Rotary said Barton is threatening to take down any businesses that don't support his mayoral bid." Jason looked like he'd tasted something bad and took a big swig of his soda.

"Roger's such a blowhard. Just ..." John stopped short. Barton sat on the Board of Directors for Johnson Manufacturing. Anger swelled in him as he thought about Bob Johnson and what must have happened as a result of all the pressure applied by vile Barton. Up to this point, John had considered the mayor to be a horrible man, unworthy of much consideration. This opinion had now been intensified.

"Well, that explains it," John said with a sigh. "We lost the Johnson account today."

"That bastard," Jason said, disgusted.

"Gwen certainly has him on the run," John said. He made a mental note about which of their other big clients might be affected by Barton's strong-arming.

"I saw coverage of the party. Man, Marsh's cousin is a knockout," Jason said, changing the subject.

At the thought of Val, the color in John's cheeks rose.

"So, how'd the party go?" Jason asked, trying to coax some details out of his friend.

"It was quite a show. Marsh and Barton argued a lot, and the mayor huffed out pretty early." John wanted to turn the conversation away from the party and especially from Val. Jason was his closest friend, but he didn't want to talk about Val yet. Unfortunately, Jason didn't take the hint.

"What's her name again? Val something? She looked amazing in that dress. Is she dating the photographer or something? She's in every one of his pictures." Jason said, finally noticing John's discomfort though not understanding it. He clumsily shifted the subject. "I bet Roger was pissed to see Gwen there."

John let himself breathe again. "Yes, though I don't know why. Gwen's a serious candidate. He's got to realize that, even if her chances of beating him are remote. He was ready to tear into her the minute he walked into the room, but Carlton didn't let things get ugly. I think the strain of being civil finally got to Roger." John paused for a moment. "I'm concerned about how vicious he's gotten lately." His brow furrowed as he thought about Barton's latest stream of public outbursts and his less-than-ethical business tactics behind the scenes.

The pair continued to discuss the party, with John talking willingly about every single guest except Val, which Jason noted with silent curiosity. After polishing off some fish and chips, the men said their goodbyes and headed back to their offices.

Returning to work with a sense of purpose, John called another meeting and soon his office was in full-on strategy mode. His staff made notes of all clients with ties to Barton, scheduled times to touch base, and made contingency plans. By the end of the day, John's sunny morning was a distant memory, and he went home seeking solace.

When he arrived at his apartment, he switched on the news and watched as he logged into his computer. Images of Saturday's party still flashed across the screen. John's frustration with Barton overrode his happiness at seeing Val's lovely form. The anchor discussed the campaign itself. Barton's smug face appeared next to Gwen's, and then the anchor cut over to a recent interview with the mayor.

"Mayor Barton, what do you think of your opponent?" the young reporter asked a smiling Barton.

"Well, I think Ms. Marsh has served the city well, but she's too green to take on this office. How many years has she been out of school? The people of Cambria need a leader who's been around. I know Cambria. And I'm willing to do whatever it takes to continue serving you."

His campaign smile looked sinister to John, and he paused the frame for a moment, studying Barton and contemplating his words. *You'll do anything to win,* John thought. *Not this year, buddy.* John sat in front of the computer and went to work.

* * *

The next day, John had readied himself for battle, but when he got to the office, all was quiet, calm. A quick check assured him the majority of their client relationships remained steady and strong. John settled in for the day, and by close of business, he was satisfied his company would survive this election.

Before leaving work, he called Val, hoping to catch her for dinner, but she planned to work late. About ready to head home, he decided that, dinner or no, he needed to see her. He picked up two coffees and headed for the Century Building.

As he drove to her office, John mused about how forward he was with Val. The self-proclaimed recluse turned downright bold in her presence, romantic even. She brought out a hidden side of him. It had become difficult to get through the days without seeing her. He liked talking to Val about nothing and everything. She was intelligent and witty, stubborn but fiery. A mystery. He suspected her father's death had affected her even more deeply than she'd been willing to admit to him, and something about that depth of sadness touched him.

John never dated. Well, almost never. He'd had a serious girl-friend in college, Suzanne, but life had pulled them in different directions, and they'd lost touch. How strange to think about that relationship now. He'd loved Suzanne's gentleness and kindness, and she seemed to understand his dark moods, his solitary nature. When they'd started drifting apart, he'd let it happen. He hadn't begged or pleaded. He simply let her go and moved forward without her. Now and then, he wondered about her, but those sorts of thoughts never lingered.

John was different with Val. They didn't really have a relationship, at least not explicitly, but already he yearned for her. Saturday night's texting had started a pattern. When he found himself thinking about her during the day, he sent her a message. And when she texted him back, he felt connected to something bigger than himself. She was intriguing.

He wanted to protect her. He wanted to see her succeed. And he wanted to be a part of her life, of her world. Val was strange, beautiful, and absolutely confounding, John was hooked.

He found Val in her office, busily typing, her hair twirled up into a bun and held in place with a pencil which had teeth marks in it. She looked up and greeted John with a warm smile, joy and surprise taking over her features. He handed her a cup of coffee, and she pushed a pile of miscellaneous papers and books off the chair next to her so he could sit down. She sipped the coffee, breathing in the aroma. "Thank you."

"Hope you don't mind me dropping by," he said, and then went out on a limb. "I missed your face."

Blood rushed to Val's cheeks. For once, she didn't mind. She'd begun to trust John, and though she was a natural blusher, she didn't feel the anxiety that usually accompanied the facial heat. "I was thinking about you," she ventured, unwilling to admit to missing him but also not wanting to appear detached. She didn't want him to think of her as cold.

Val discussed her client work and campaign promotions. She spoke with fervor and said she found it deeply satisfying. John told her about his week so far, including his lost contract, when he noticed her face had gone pale.

"Are you all right?" He reached out to touch her arm. She shifted away distractedly, and stood to look out the window.

"Roger Barton scares me," she admitted. "The idea that he might stoop so low to win this election scares me. This is why

I've avoided working in politics." Her stress level rose, and John could feel her emotionally pull away from him.

"He's just a lot of hot air." John stood, moving closer to Val.

She turned to face him. "Look, John, I have a lot of work to do. I really appreciate the coffee, but I need to get back to it." She moved past him and walked toward the door, giving him no alternative except to leave.

"Can we have lunch tomorrow?" he said hopefully, his feelings a bit bruised by the brush-off.

"I can't. I'm meeting with a client," she said, leaving no room for further discussion. Dejected, he kissed her lightly on the cheek, said goodbye, and drove home, reeling from the unexpected turn of events.

* * *

After he left, Val slumped in her chair, near tears without clearly understanding the reason. The rush of exhilaration she had when John walked in, followed closely with the fear at hearing about Barton's latest angry antics, made Val's head spin. The old familiar panic set in. Val thought about her business, how hard she'd worked to make things the way she liked them. And then she got involved in this campaign, and John walked into her life. Her breathing came in ragged gasps as she tried to tame the anxiety that crept over her, taking hold of her rational mind and adding too many wild, obsessive ponderings.

She put her head down on her desk, took deep breaths, and tried to think of nothing. When she finally allowed herself to sit upright, she saw the cup of coffee, ignored, cooling down. And she reminded herself that Barton's behavior wasn't John's fault. Packing up for the day, Val felt off-kilter and wondered what the future would bring. Sleep certainly wouldn't come easily. She prepared for a long night.

* * *

The next morning, a particularly nasty post on Jabber railed against Barton with little mention of Gwen. At lunch, Gwen and Val discussed the post. The blogger had called Barton out on his less than professional behavior, noting his barely concealed animosity toward his opponent and challenging the mayor to meet Gwen in open debate. Still two months to go in the campaign, the blogger set the stage for the first in a series of face-offs they were sure would be brutal.

Gwen believed she could gain ground in the election through the debates. She counted on Barton's arrogance and impulsiveness, his inability to control himself. A master debater at college, Gwen relished an opportunity to take Barton on. She was calm and composed, but cunning. She and Val agreed a debate was the thing her campaign needed.

After a few minutes of campaign talk, Gwen shifted topics. "So, what about the photographer?"

Val groaned. "I'm not even remotely interested in the photographer, Gwen," she said, hoping the conversation would end. Fat chance.

"Why not? He's adorable!" Gwen squeaked. "And clearly into you. I mean, you made front page news." Gwen shot Val a playful smile, referring to the non-stop streaming that had graced the local news all weekend.

"Yes, *he* was definitely interested," Val said. "But I'm not, so that's that."

"What about John?" Gwen asked, and seeing the color rise in Val's cheeks, she knew she'd hit pay dirt. "Where did he run off to Saturday night?"

"Actually, I'm not sure he ever told me where he went," Val said, thinking back on their conversations.

"You've talked to him since then?" Gwen asked, curiosity clearly showing on her face.

"We had coffee Sunday," Val said, hesitating, "and then again last night." She knew there would be no end to Gwen's interrogation now.

"Oh, my God, Val. Are we even friends anymore? How dare

you not tell me about this!" Gwen bubbled over with excitement, and Val realized she might as well come clean.

"I like him a lot," said Val simply, feeling exposed even with Gwen. "He's amazing, and I think about him practically non-stop, and it's going to end in disaster." She allowed herself a moment to pout.

"What in the world are you talking about?" Gwen asked, seeing her cousin shutting down, despair creeping up in her voice.

"He told me he lost a client because of Barton," Val said, hoping Gwen would understand her meaning without dredging up all the details. "I can't do all of this, Gwen. Politics. Love. I can't handle it all at once!" Desperate tears formed in Val's eyes. Gwen got up and scooted in next to Val, snuggling up against her cousin.

"It's going to be okay. You're not your dad. Neither is John. I know this scares the hell out of you, but I promise, it's going to work out." Gwen talked softly and soothingly to Val, something that always made her feel better.

"Oh, Gwen," Val said, exhaling deeply and letting go of her stress. "Relationships don't work for me. I can't let myself go enough. I seriously wish I could because John is unlike any man I've ever met."

She thought about the look on his face when she kicked him out of her office the previous evening and felt a horrible twinge of guilt. She never wanted to cause someone else's pain or disappointment, especially his.

"You can't shut everyone out forever," Gwen said, still resting her cheek on Val's shoulder. "For heaven's sake, you've got the reclusive John Hatfield coming out of hiding to see you. He must think you're pretty amazing, too." Gwen handled Val expertly. Feeling her cousin's shoulders relax, Gwen slipped back over to her own side of the booth and took another bite of her salad.

Val sipped tea and took a few more moments to regain her composure before picking up the conversation again. Gwen left her alone now on the subject of men, but she vowed not to let Val withdraw or talk herself out of love before it even had a chance to get off the ground.

The girls wrapped up their meal and walked back to Val's office. As Val opened the door, someone called, "Val Shakely?"

She turned, and a delivery-man carrying an enormous vase of flowers – stargazer lilies, roses, and baby's breath flowing out in all directions – strode up to her. Gwen grabbed the door so Val could take the flowers. She placed them on her desk and opened the card. It read, "Dinner? Pretty please? Eight o'clock at Maude's?"

Val smiled and Gwen snatched the card out of her hand. Reading it, she beamed. "Let's go shopping!" Without waiting for an objection, she grabbed Val's purse and headed out the door.

* * *

Val walked into Maude's wearing yet another new dress, making this the most absurdly girly period of her life. John waited inside, handsome as ever, and he sucked in some breath when he saw Val walk toward him. Her red dress was far more revealing than anything she had ever picked out on her own, but between Gwen and the flowers, she'd been more pliable than usual.

"Wow! You're stunning," John said, as he offered Val his arm.

She took it and smiled a thank you, gazing into his eyes a bit longer than necessary. She enjoyed seeing him squirm for a change.

They followed the host to a table which overlooked the river. Maude's was fine dining, quaint and private. The lights glowed dimly and candles adorned each table to create a romantic atmosphere. The space was long and narrow, each table separated by a tall divider, giving every party a sense of seclusion.

They ordered wine and talked about their day. It was a relief to enjoy some small talk and closeness. John reached across the table to take Val's hand, and while they talked, he stroked her fingers playfully. Gwen had lectured Val all the way home about giving this relationship a chance and Val promised she'd try. She wanted to. During pauses in the conversation, she gazed out the window to see the autumn moon glitter off the water.

"Val?"

She looked up and realized she'd been completely lost in thought. John looked at her inquisitively.

"What are you thinking about?" he asked, genuinely interested.

"My parents, actually," she said, somewhat self-consciously but determined not to put her guard up with John. "When my father lost his business, he lost himself. My mother never forgave him, I think, for not seeing past his losses. I never thought about it until today, but I think I'm starting to comprehend how she might have reacted. She was there for him through everything, but he wasn't there for her at the end." She looked sadly at John, and he squeezed her hand, wanting to comfort her, to take away her sorrow.

"My father and I never seemed to see eye-to-eye," he said, reflecting. "He and my mother never had a stellar relationship though they put on an excellent show in public, and with me ... well, I was never good enough to garner much attention. Even when I took over the business, the support never seemed to be there." He looked pained. "I always wanted him to be proud of me."

The arrival of their meals interrupted the conversation, and they ate in silence, stealing glances at one another and contemplating the evening. The mood lightened with time, and by the end, they chatted amiably again.

"Do you want to take a walk down by the water?" John asked, looking hopefully at Val.

"Sure," she said, glad she'd brought her heavy dress coat.

Cambria Riverfront Walk was a popular spot for couples. In the fall, the breeze off the river usually made it too cold for everyone except the hardiest or most passionate lovers. John took Val's hand, and they walked down the boardwalk, passing only a few people here and there as they went. A few blocks from the restaurant, an overlook with benches provided respite. Tonight, it was deserted. John pulled Val toward the bench that seemed most likely to be shielded from the breeze and they sat down close together, using the cold as an excuse to hold each other. John wrapped his arms around Val and she rested her head on his chest, feeling his breathing become slow and long.

"I could stay like this all night," she murmured, surprised to hear the words coming so easily. His breathing sped up and hers followed. Raising her head to see his face, she met his gaze. He stared down at her with such intensity that she could feel the warmth and energy of his look permeate her body. He leaned down and kissed her on the lips. His were impossibly soft and she melted, wrapping her arms around his neck and running her hands through his hair as she kissed him back passionately.

When he finally broke away from her, his breath ragged, he leaned close to her ear and said, "I've been wanting to kiss you like that for days." She could hear the smile on his lips. His voice, low and sultry, sent chills down her spine. She closed her eyes again, willing the moment to last. He didn't pull back. Instead, he tentatively kissed her neck near her ear, running his hands down her back. His breaths came soft and fast, and they stayed like that for what seemed like forever. She shivered and he realized it had gotten bitterly cold. He kissed her softly on the forehead and then helped her up, putting his arm around her as they walked back toward the restaurant.

When they reached Val's car, John wrapped his arms around her and kissed her again, this time slowly, gently. She clung to him, pushing her body into his, and he held her tightly until they reluctantly pulled apart. She climbed behind the wheel. As she pulled away from the curb, he stood, hands jammed in his pockets, watching her go. She could feel his eyes on her as she drove away.

CHAPTER 7

With the weekend approaching, Val worked hard on her many client projects. As she prepared press releases for the first debate, a call came in. It was Margery Stovall, a long-time friend and client. Margery exchanged pleasantries with Val, who wondered about the point of the call.

"Val, sweetheart, you've always done a wonderful job for us. But I'm afraid we're going to have to take a break from working with you."

Val nearly dropped the phone. "Have I done something wrong?" Val stammered, her mind racing. She'd worked with Margery for nearly five years without a hiccup.

"Honestly, Val, there's too much pressure on our organization right now. Roger Barton is our landlord, and we don't want to get involved in the politics."

Val's heart fell. Barton was pressuring them and, despite her good record, she had lost this client. How many others would follow suit?

"Isn't there anything I can do to change your mind?" Val said, her voice thick with desperation.

"I'll call you after the election, dear," Margery said, and she hung up.

Val sat, stunned, for a long time. Her mind, which normally would have set straight away into resolution mode, remained stuck in an endless loop of fear and despair. She could hear her father's voice on the phone, cracking, as he told her about shutting his business down. As much as she tried to overcome it, she was terrified of the effect of local politics on her business. Her breathing got ragged until she felt like she was going to pass out.

Val knew her feelings might be overblown, but that awareness did her no good at the moment. Since she began on Gwen's campaign, Val had thought a lot about her father and started to suspect her memories of his situation might be skewed due to her feelings for him. That didn't stop the panic from coming in waves, and even trying to talk to herself rationally about things had little effect on taming her feelings.

It occurred to her in moments like these she probably needed to see her therapist again. It couldn't be normal to live in this state of constant fear. Instead of addressing it head-on, she merely altered the entire course of her life in a wide arc around trouble. She didn't take on controversial clients. She never made the newspapers, deliberately taking a back seat when credit got handed out. She kept far behind the scenes, and she loved it that way. It was secure. Now, in a reversal, she experienced terror at the hands of some crummy local politician, saw herself on the news, and dated one of the biggest targets in Cambria!

Breathe, Val, she thought and gulped in some much-needed oxygen to calm herself. *You're getting hysterical.* She was thankful she worked alone. She was free to lay her head down on her desk and wallow in self-pity for an extraordinarily long time without anyone catching a glimpse of her pathetic state.

Eventually, she calmed down and organized her thoughts. She made a list of all the clients she thought might have ties to Barton and spent the rest of the day making friendly phone calls to check in. By the end of the day she relaxed as she'd gotten most of them on the phone.

Before leaving, she checked Jabber, finding nothing new about the campaign. Val avoided thinking about the election all day, preferring to focus instead on her regular clients. Now, she thought about Gwen and how much she admired her cousin's fearlessness. She needed a dose of that right about now. Val had taken on a risky and challenging campaign, and when she didn't feel terrified, she was exhilarated. It had been much more fun than she had ever thought it would be. Her stress level had risen significantly. Her sleep suffered and she couldn't concentrate with her normal, single-minded determination. Of course, some of that had to do with the campaign and some of that had to do with John.

He'd been unusually quiet today, though she'd only noticed it toward close of business due to the frustration of her own workday. For the past few days, he'd texted her pretty frequently – every day, in fact. Val expected to hear from him by now and was surprised at how disappointed his silence left her feeling. Okay, maybe not *that* surprising. She thought about his arms around her and his lips, soft and hungry on hers. Suddenly, longing replaced her disappointment.

It finally drove her to action. She texted him. *Hey you, what are you doing?*

Her phone buzzed almost immediately. *Waiting to walk you home.*

Her heart literally skipped a beat. She opened her office door. In one step, John strode through the doorway, held her face for a moment in his hands, and kissed her. The world faded away, and she was lost in the kiss. His arms slid around her back and held her close while his mouth explored hers.

Finally pulling away, she asked him, "How long were you out there?"

"Just a little while." His voice was husky, his breath coming in fits and starts as he tried visibly to compose himself.

"Well, I planned on packing up. It's been an awful day, and I can't wait to get out of here."

Val moved toward her desk, put things in their respective

places, gathered her jacket and purse, and gave John a nuts-and-bolts overview of her conversation with Margery. John tried to comfort her, but she could see his mind turn inward, pondering something, a frown creeping onto his face.

They exited, hand in hand, into the chilly autumn evening. With John, Val remained in a constant state of flux. It appeared natural to be with him, but the sensations that stirred were unfamiliar, unsettling. She was never entirely comfortable, which she interpreted as a sign of impending doom.

As a general rule, Val sought out the comfortable path in all things. Not that she feared a challenge, but as confident as she was with her career, she was equally unsure of her personal life. She'd never stood up for herself. She was a people pleaser, and she used that quality to avoid situations where she might need to take a stand. She was diplomatic but also easily overlooked. With John, she wasn't her usual self.

John held the door when they reached her apartment building. They said their goodbyes, and though the temptation nearly suffocated her, she didn't invite him in. Somehow, bringing him into her safest, most personal sanctuary seemed too overwhelming under the current circumstances. She watched him walk away and then took the stairs up to her apartment.

She made herself a cup of tea and stretched out on the couch. A storm raged inside her. She couldn't shake the feeling that the decision to work with Gwen would be the downfall of everything she'd worked for in her professional life. Her fear, combined with the outrage that one man could have such a negative effect on her life despite all her good work, made her feel crazy, out-of-whack. Nothing scared Val more than uncertainty.

And then ... John. Since the day Val had crossed paths with him, she'd been in a state of constant turmoil. She was falling in love with him and not completely happy about the turn of events. Being with John was like discovering an exciting, uncharted country – new and strange and wonderful. In a matter of weeks,

Val had gone from focusing almost every thought on work to finding herself constantly distracted by thoughts of John. The stupid grin that overtook her whole face at the mere thought of him was embarrassing.

Life had gone complex, and as much as Val considered herself a mature adult, she found the new state of affairs suffocating. It reduced her to childish fears. She found herself thinking constantly about her father and her family. She'd always blamed her father's decline, and ultimate death, on the failure of his business. She began to spiral downward and feel his pain more acutely. She also wondered if there was more to the story.

After her father died, Val had sought out a therapist to help her sort through the grief. It had taken only two visits before she realized this woman would make her look into scary and unfamiliar places in her soul, and so she quit going.

During her last visit, the therapist had suggested Val's father might have suffered from a deeper and clinical depression. Considering this possibility represented a betrayal to Val, and she'd never given the comment a second thought, until now.

Val wondered whether blaming her mother for abandoning her father had been unfair. She'd never allowed her mother to talk about him, refusing to hear another side of the story than the one adopted as truth. Avoidance had been simple, manageable. Now, as she considered things she wasn't prepared to deal with, and she wondered if she too couldn't face the reality in front of her.

Val groaned, loudly. She switched on the TV to see a smiling photo of Gwen beside Barton's sneering face. The reporter pointed out that Gwen's numbers had crept up in the polls. She ended the segment with the statement, "Mayor Barton must be feeling the pressure now."

Barton certainly acknowledged the pressure and he lashed out, first at John's company and now at Val's. Every nightmarish thought she ever had about local politics immediately seemed true, and stirrings of regret about having put herself in the line of fire began to emerge. She saw her quiet life, one she'd worked so hard to build and maintain, go up in flames.

The news switched to sports, and Val closed her eyes, resting her head against the back of the couch. She dozed for a while before dragging herself to bed for a night of fitful sleep.

* * *

John headed home with thoughts of Barton and the impact his rash behavior had on Val. The man was out of control. His erratic and unprofessional behavior had become problematic for both of them. Barton used his power to attack people for purely selfish reasons.

While John deplored Barton's actions toward his own business, he knew it would survive. This new strike on Val's business had him livid. For a moment, he allowed himself a smirk, amused at the fact his emotions concerning Val were so much bigger than anything he'd ever felt before.

John made his way directly to his apartment's couch and got back to his musings. Val was going to be a big complication in his life. When he'd walked her home, he could see anxiety and panic written all over her face and posture. She flip-flopped between opening herself up to him and shutting him out. John could see her freaking out about Barton and he knew Val wasn't the kind of girl who let things go easily.

On one hand, John understood that the election and his distaste for Barton had led him to attend Gwen's launch party. If he'd avoided that party like he did practically every other social engagement, he might never have met Val.

The memory of their first encounter brought a smile to his lips. He'd regretted his decision to attend, locked into a boring conversation with some men from the Chamber of Commerce, when his attention momentarily shifted to a woman across the room. He met her eyes, realizing she'd stared at him, not a huge surprise. John made so few appearances in public that, when he did show his face, he expected to be stalked by press or some businessperson he'd been deftly avoiding. When she'd gestured to her purse and his tie, he'd had to choke back a laugh. Getting caught in his distraction, John told his colleagues about the exchange, and when they'd looked, she turned red and darted through the crowd.

Her sudden disappearance piqued his curiosity. He couldn't understand why she'd draw attention to herself and then run away. So John had excused himself from the group and tracked the mystery woman down, nearly bumping into her at the water table.

His first conversation with Val was awkward and infuriating, but it did nothing to alleviate his curiosity. Now, after having gotten to know her, he realized how uncharacteristic that moment had been. Val's normal state of being was shy and reserved, she was incredibly careful not to attract undue attention to herself. John couldn't help but be thankful for her momentary lapse in control that evening.

John's phone rang, returning him to the present, and he found himself with plans for the evening.

* * *

He and his brother David met downtown at one of their favorite sports bars to watch the game and have dinner. Walking through the noisy bar area toward their table, John took a deep breath, ready for a distraction from his non-stop contemplation. He and David ordered drinks and burgers and watched the game for a few minutes in silence.

Finally, David looked over at John and said, "So, you look pretty frazzled. What's going on?"

"A lot, actually," John said, noting his brother's raised eyebrows. John's low-profile, homebody life didn't often result in much drama, so David was clearly surprised by the response.

"Okay," David said hesitantly when John didn't continue. "Do I have to drag it out of you?"

John smiled, "I'm trying to decide where to start." He took another breath and finally dove in. "A few weeks ago, I decided to go to Gwen Marsh's campaign party. The result? I lost a huge client and am possibly falling in love."

David choked on his beer. "Love?"

"What? Losing a client doesn't surprise you?" John joked. "Yes, I met someone. Her name is Val, and I'm falling in love. She's amazing and scary and beautiful and frustrating, and I think about her pretty much constantly."

David smiled. For all of his brother's no-nonsense style, he could sure be a drama queen. "She sounds wonderful and awful."

John chuckled. "Oh, she is. She's guarded. Sometimes I think she loves me, too, and sometimes I think she'd like me to get the hell out of her life." John sighed. "And then there's Barton."

"Oh, no. Not Roger!" David grinned knowingly. "What's he up to these days?"

"As you might suspect, he pretty much hates Gwen Marsh. But his behavior has been ridiculous even for him." John described Barton's visit to his office, the loss of the Johnson account, and the jabs at Gwen at the governor's dinner.

"Well, we all know Barton's a hothead," said David, taking another sip of his beer. "Although, bullying other businesses based on his political aspirations dips pretty low even for him."

"Yeah, I know. His outbursts are all over the place. And Val mentioned she lost a client today because *they're* under political pressure. I did some research and found that Roger's company is not only their landlord, but also one of their financial backers. A quick phone call confirmed their funding was threatened if they continued to work with Val because of her political ties."

At this, David raised his eyebrows.

"Hmm. This is starting to sound suspiciously like an ethics violation." Judge David was now in full professional mode. "Isn't that foundation a city sponsored organization? I can't imagine that Barton applying political pressure to a group that receives city funding would be condoned."

John considered this new angle. He shrugged, "It's a mess. He has Val scared to death. She's run her business on her own for years, and she's worried he's going to sink her. And she might be right. That's what happened to her father's business back when Jim Bradley ran for city council, apparently." John watched the wheels turning in his brother's brain.

"Well, steer clear of Roger if you can. You might think about reporting him to the Colorado Independent Ethics Commission. There's no reason to tolerate his behavior, and even if he's not in direct violation, they might give him a warning he'll feel inclined to follow," David said.

"We'll see how it goes," John said.

He and David finished off their first round of beers, gobbled down their burgers, and spent the rest of the evening engaged in the game. John felt better having confided in his brother. Talking about Val made the whole relationship seem less crazy, more real.

Midway through the game, Jason showed up. The three men whooped and hollered and left the restaurant a few hours later, happy with their team's win. It was almost normal. Just the boys, hanging out, watching the game. But when John got home, he found himself immersed in thoughts about Val.

CHAPTER 8

The weekend went by in a blur of activity, and though Val spent a good deal of time thinking about John, the hectic pace of debate prep made it impossible to connect in person. Despite the pressure, Gwen portrayed a picture of serenity. She kept things moving and never seemed to lose her cool.

Questions had been emailed to the candidates for the debate, sponsored by the Cambria Women Republicans. Val had spent most of the weekend at Gwen's house where she, campaign manager Victoria, and a small handful of volunteers and staffers helped to prepare for the main event. Gwen was a natural, and Val often found herself listening with rapt attention as her cousin smoothly crafted answers to even the most obtuse questions.

Val had prepared press releases and arranged interviews with the local media outlets. Leading up to Tuesday's debate, Gwen and Val would be completely consumed. Val put the finishing touches on the campaign's social media posts for the day, engaging the online audience and impressed with the results. Questions and words of encouragement poured in, and Gwen took time to respond to all of them. Val wondered when the girl got any sleep.

The debate format included a question and answer period for the second half of the allotted time, and the public questions Gwen received on her website and social media pages proved critical in helping her prepare. Val also monitored Internet and broadcast media outlets for news on Barton in an attempt to head any problems off at the pass. Most of the comments under Barton's social media pages tended to focus on Gwen's gender and youth as primary targets for criticism, so Val and Gwen prepared answers for those as well.

Val researched Cambria politics, identifying the city's youngest politicians and making note of their accomplishments while in office. She and Gwen became intimately familiar with every woman who'd ever held a prominent role in Cambrian politics and society, arming themselves with a body of knowledge designed to combat Barton's expected cheap shots.

By Monday morning, the Gwen's campaign stood ready. Val and her cousin hit the first of three radio interviews for the day, followed immediately by an interview with the local newspaper. The radio spots went quickly, but the newspaper reporter took an extraordinary amount of time covering even the minutest details of Gwen's life and campaign. Gwen took the interrogation in stride, though it left Val feeling vulnerable. Val made copious notes on topics she wanted to research further.

She had to admit Gwen performed like a pro. She never appeared flustered or disturbed by any questions, and by the end of the interview, she and the reporter chatted like lifelong friends.

Val thought about work the whole time. She took notes about the interview, brainstorming ideas for blog posts and social media blasts based on Gwen's answers and on any patterns or trends she noted in the reporter's queries. She made follow-up notes for her contacts at local media outlets, including even the most obscure independent blogs and news sites. She'd aimed to get Gwen in front of every single source she could muster, especially those that catered to Cambria's younger demographic who tended to make up the majority of independent voters – a coveted group in this nonpartisan election.

Val wondered if it might be worth reaching out to Jabber, though she knew attempts to do so by other public relations outlets had been ignored. For the first time since Gwen had announced her candidacy, Val started thinking about her cousin's chances of winning as more than a pipe dream.

At lunch, Val wanted to talk strategy, but Gwen had her sights on another topic.

"So, when do *we* see John next?" she asked Val as if they were partners discussing an important business deal.

Val smiled. "*We* aren't sure. Ask me after the debate is over and *we* can breathe again."

John had texted Val every day since their "walk home" date but had kept the conversation casual, which Val appreciated greatly given her hectic schedule. Now that the topic had turned to John, she realized how much she hoped to hear from him.

"I think maybe *we* should take a look behind us then," Gwen chuckled.

Val gulped down her mouthful of tea and turned around slowly. And there he stood. Val smiled so hard her cheeks hurt.

John walked to her table, leaned close to her ear, and whispered, "Had to see you today in the flesh." His breath blew hot on Val's ear, sending tingles down her neck and spine. "Didn't want you to believe I wasn't thinking about you."

He looked up, sheepishly, across the table and said "Hello, Gwen." Then he noticed quite a few other diners had looked in his direction.

Val's face turned red as a beet. Her romance with John had gone from theoretical to front-page news in a big way. She still faced him, and she whispered, her voice ragged, "You sure make a scene for such a private person." Noticing his discomfort as the center of attention, Val giggled softly. "Are you following me, Mr. Hatfield?"

"Could be," he said, and without another word, he brushed his lips against her cheek and left the restaurant. Only a second or two later, Val's phone buzzed. A text from John: *Can I walk you home?*

Willing the stupid grin from her face, she texted back a quick *Yes* and attempted to get back to business. But the damage was done. The restaurant buzzed and Val caught people glancing over at her. Her cheeks seemed destined to stay in a perpetual state of fire engine red. She and Gwen finished up as quickly as they could and headed to her office in search of refuge.

When they got there, Gwen said, grinning mischievously, "So, *is* he stalking you?"

Val laughed. "Honestly, I don't know. I'm not sure how he finds me."

"That man is in love with you," Gwen said, confident in her powers of observation.

"Oh, it's so much worse than that. I think I'm falling in love with him." Almost as soon as the words had left her mouth, Val regretted revealing so much. Uttering the words out loud seemed like giving away too much.

Gwen took a long, deep, and overly dramatic breath and said, simply, "Duh."

Val relaxed a little. "Can we get back to work, please?"

Gwen left an hour later with a list of contacts to make, and Val scheduled interviews for the rest of the day. She reached out to reporters she knew, and submitted final pre-debate press releases. She updated Gwen's website, put out a last call for questions on her Facebook page, and prepared to log off when a knock sounded at the door. Expecting John, she said, "Come in," and was surprised to find Constance Carlton there instead.

"Constance! How are you? I didn't expect to see you," Val said, walking to the door to greet her guest.

"I had an appointment elsewhere in the building and decided to stop by. I heard an interesting rumor today."

Val immediately jumped to the wrong conclusion and was even more startled when Constance held out her phone to reveal a charming and completely candid picture of John kissing the cheek of a woman who looked suspiciously like Val.

"Oh, my God!" Val nearly shouted. She snatched the phone from Constance's hand and scrolled down. The caption read, *Looks like Cambria's most eligible bachelor is off the market!*

Val sank down in a chair, her heart racing. It was like being a celebrity stalked by paparazzi, uncomfortable and exposed, like a dream where you're giving a speech and discover you don't have any clothes on.

Constance walked over to Val's desk, pulled up another chair, and laughed. "For heaven's sake, Val. It's just a little romance. No one died."

Val handed Constance her phone and took a deep breath. She *was* behaving badly, but it was all new territory. Daylight glimmered on the horizon. Dating John meant a loss of the privacy and anonymity Val had grown accustomed to. *Ugh,* she thought.

"What site was that on?" Val asked.

"The Daily Blast. They're notoriously nosy." As the governor's wife, Constance had gotten used to the cameras. "Now, I think you'd better give me the scoop."

Val sighed and gave Constance highlights of her budding romance. Constance smiled broadly. "You know, you and John may be perfect for each other."

Val smiled too. "He's amazing, but I wish I didn't feel so blindsided by the whole thing. He puts me off-balance."

"Love's not easy, darling," Constance said, "and loving a … um … newsworthy man takes some getting used to. Look at it this way, Val – you're a good person and so is John. I can't say I know him well, but I think he avoids controversy the way you do, so once the novelty wears off, they'll move on to more interesting prospects." She stood to leave. "Now that I've riled you, I've got to get home." As she opened the door, she almost walked into John, his hand raised to knock.

"Mrs. Carlton," he said, politely, holding the door for her.

"Mr. Hatfield." She looked back at Val, winked, and said, "You two have a lovely evening."

John moved aside as Constance walked out the door and down the hall. Then he sat down beside Val's desk and tried to puzzle out the expression on her face. He reached out to touch her hand, and she snatched his up rather hungrily, the physical connection making her feel more grounded.

"Hi," she said, her voice still shaky from shock. She felt like a huge baby, so easily startled by every little thing.

"Are you okay?" he asked, his voice riddled with concern.

"I'm fine. Just startled." She smiled at him for reassurance. "Looks like we've been discovered." He looked at her quizzically. A quick search on her phone revealed the damning picture, and she handed it to him.

He chuckled, looking more than a little uncomfortable. "I guess so."

"It seems weird that some stranger took a picture and posted it online," she complained, though without much force behind her words. The shock had worn off and, other than feeling somewhat irritated, she regained her composure.

"Yes, I realize I've brought this on myself, and you unfortunately, by being such a hermit." He sighed and squeezed Val's hand tighter.

"Constance broke the news to me in pretty dramatic fashion," Val chuckled, feeling ridiculous now about her reaction. "If it means I have to be stalked to be with you, I'll take it." She leaned in to kiss John's cheek. He blushed, and she laughed out loud; the tables had turned.

She packed up the rest of her things, put on her coat, and they headed out for the walk home. A slight breeze prompted her to snuggle up next to him while they walked, chatting about the weather, the city lights, and any other meaningless topic she could think of. They walked slowly, savoring the time together, all too aware of how short the distance was. When they arrived at Val's building, John pulled her close and kissed her long and slow, unwilling to let her body move even the slightest bit away from his. Val could think of nothing but John – the feel of his strong arms pulling her to him and the way his hair fell over his eyes as he bent to meet her lips.

She said, huskily, "Do you want to come up and maybe watch a movie?" She looked up, and a wave of disappointment washed over her. She could see the answer would be no.

"I'd love to, but I told my mother I'd come for coffee tonight." He looked positively conflicted

Val conceded, "Don't worry. I probably need to get some rest before tomorrow. We've got a handful of interviews scheduled and then the debate. Are you going?"

"Wouldn't miss it," John said enthusiastically. He looked forward to watching Barton squirm.

"I'll see you there."

As she turned to walk inside, she hesitated. A feeling of loss swept through her. Instead of walking away, she threw herself back into John's arms, taking him by surprise. She wrapped her arms around his neck and kissed him hard, willing her body to meld with his, never wanting to let go.

When she finally did let go, he looked into her eyes and said, "When I met you, I didn't know how much you would change my life." He smiled, his face glowing with affection.

Her breath caught and she let the warmth of his words flow through her. He kissed her lightly on the cheek, promised to see her on Tuesday, and walked away.

CHAPTER 9

Tuesday morning was cold and hazy. Sluggishly, Val hit the snooze on her alarm as many times as she could reasonably get away with. The final time the buzzing didn't stop, and it took her a while to realize it was her phone. She picked it up. 7:36. Gwen had already texted her about their first morning interview. Before answering, Val took a few moments to sit up, stretch, and take a hot shower.

By the time Val got dressed, Gwen had texted seven more times. Her cousin sounded uncharacteristically, though understandably, anxious. At the last moment, they'd landed Gwen an interview with the local cable news program. An unexpected television appearance generated the need for extra preparation, so Gwen was up and at 'em early.

Val met her cousin at Java Lite, and they rode together to the television studio. She prepped Gwen as they waited for airtime, getting primped by the program's makeup artists, and sipping on coffee. When Gwen went on air, Val watched behind the monitors, noting how confident Gwen looked and how easily she built rapport with the hosts. The interview was a huge success. When asked about Barton's attack on her youth and lack of experience, Gwen gave an extensive list of *her* accomplishments and then followed it with a list of some of Cambria's most accomplished women, many of whom she knew would be watching the show.

Val grinned. The hosts nodded, agreeing eagerly with Gwen, and by the end of the segment, even the male host said, "There's no doubt women have shaped the political landscape of Cambria." The interview ended strongly, and as they left the studio, Gwen's phone went crazy. She spent the next half hour returning calls and texts as they headed back to Val's car and the next interview.

After a late lunch, Val returned to her office for a few hours of downtime before the debate. She'd created several press releases anticipating different outcomes. She'd choose one to send at the start of the debate once she had a better idea of how things would go, hoping to make the media outlets the next morning. She also worked on other client projects she'd neglected over the last few days.

She pulled up her email and began reading. About three messages in, Val came across one from the president of the board of directors for one of her civic groups. They exchanged emails nearly every day, but Val was unprepared for what she read. She was being asked to step down.

She re-read the message several times before it finally sunk in. It hinted that Val's involvement in Gwen's campaign presented a conflict of interest and the organization couldn't retain a member whose activities and affiliations might be damaging.

A queasiness consumed Val. A quick call confirmed her suspicion. The organization had received a call from Barton & Co. threatening to cut off financial support as long as Val remained on the board. Val made half-hearted pleas that fell on seemingly deaf ears. She hung up the phone and cried for the first time in more than ten years.

Both furious and crestfallen, she cycled between rage at Barton's gall and her mounting fear. She'd worked so hard for the Community Foundation, and they'd given her up without a fight. She tried to look at things rationally. She knew Barton's company was a large donor, and she tried to forgive the foundation for falling to such pressure, but she simply couldn't.

Val's phone buzzed, interrupting her thoughts. Gwen was on her way over. Val wiped her eyes and sat still, focusing on breathing. It was in this unmoving state that Gwen found her ten minutes later.

"Dear God, what happened?" she exclaimed.

Val gave her cousin a quick rundown, and Gwen's face lit up with fury. "That man is unbelievable!" she cried. Her voice became high-pitched with anger, fists tightly clenched. Val rarely saw Gwen lose her cool. She hated to admit it, but it made her feel good to see it now.

"This will keep happening until I'm off the campaign, Gwen." She looked at her cousin, defeated, wanting nothing more than to walk home and hide out.

"It's going to be okay, Val." Gwen's words fell flat. She still fumed, and the defeated look on Val's face fueled her anger.

"No, it's not, Gwen. It's exactly why I don't get involved in politics," Val said. She took another deep breath and looked at Gwen. She could see her cousin's concern.

"I think, after tonight, I need to step back," she said, guilty saying this to Gwen right before the debate, but anxiety had taken over.

"Come on, Val. Please don't let Barton bully you." Gwen grew more agitated. Val knew quitting the campaign would be a blow, and she hated saying it, but she was desperate.

"Try to understand, Gwen. If you lose this campaign, you'll still go back to your old position. If I lose my business, I lose myself." Val had always had a flair for the dramatic despite her mousy demeanor.

"Val, I refuse to let you quit. You'll learn to stand up for yourself if I have to make you!" Gwen pulled Val into a fierce hug. Val needed the contact, and she finally calmed down. Gwen was right. She needed to stand up to Barton but she wasn't comfortable with confrontation.

"Anyway, you don't have to do anything tonight except be my

cheerleader," Gwen said, turning the conversation to something more manageable.

"Okay. But I want to talk more about this tomorrow," Val said, shutting her office for the evening.

* * *

The debate took place at Town Hall, an old movie theater renovated to host live events. The stadium seating was still intact, but a stage had been erected to accommodate performances. It had become a regular venue for political debates and public speakers. When Gwen and Val arrived forty-five minutes prior to the debate, half of the six hundred seats were already filled.

A table at the entrance held cards for people to write questions on, and a line had formed. Gwen gave Val's hand a squeeze and headed toward the stage to find Agatha Brown, head of the Republican Women and moderator for the debate. Val got in line to submit a question about ethical campaigning that had been brewing in her mind for hours. She might not face Barton head-on, but she couldn't wait to hear his take on ethics in front of a large crowd and on camera.

Val searched for John but didn't see him. She said a handful of hellos and headed to the front of the auditorium to find a seat on the aisle to keep her view of the candidates unobstructed. Ten minutes before the program's start, every seat was taken and people crowded around the back of the auditorium. John still hadn't appeared, and Val was hugely disappointed as the seat she'd been unofficially saving was taken.

Brown took the stage, introduced herself, and gave a veritable sermon about the responsibility to vote in this election. Though her speech aimed at bipartisanship, a few carefully chosen notes about her organization gave the entire summation a noticeable partisan slant. The tone continued as she introduced the candidates. Gwen's introduction was factual and brief while Barton's was in-depth. Brown could barely contain the smile that kept threatening to break out on her face.

Though predictable, Val couldn't help but groan, which garnered a few reproachful looks from the people sitting next to her. Val had served on the Community Foundation's board with Brown and found her mostly intolerable. Brown was exuberant in forwarding the Republican Women's political agenda, even in an inappropriate time and place. Brown plugged her organization at every board meeting, despite the stated nonpartisan mission of the organization. Val shot her neighbors a quick smile and returned her focus to the debate.

The debate's first half consisted of questions prepared ahead of time by the event sponsors. The candidates took turns discussing fiscal management, personnel issues, sexual harassment, the relationship between the mayor and council, and more topics aimed at establishing their platforms and stances on basic administrative issues. Barton spoke smugly, noting his current experience at least twice for every response and making sure to point out the accomplishments of the city, regardless of whether or not he had any hand in those accomplishments.

Gwen's responses incorporated her four years of experience on council as well as comments about moving forward, citing other similarly sized cities' experiences, careful to note the things that made Cambria a unique community. Her answers were clear, factual, yet started to sound scripted next to Barton's folksier speech.

Val gritted her teeth several times as Barton managed to avoid answering questions completely but still got mass applause by appealing to emotions – politics as usual.

At the mid-point, the candidates were given a break, and the moderator encouraged the audience to turn in any last-minute questions. During the break, Gwen came to find Val.

"How's it sounding down here?" Gwen looked more flustered than usual.

"You're polished, but I think Barton reached the crowd better. You need to use the next section to show your personality,"

Val said, hoping not to make her cousin nervous. In true Gwen-fashion, the criticism supplied the right fuel. Val could see the wheels start to spin as Gwen formulated a plan for the next round. They chatted for a few more minutes before Gwen went in search of the ladies' room and a bottle of water. Val scanned the crowd once again, but no John. She settled back in her chair glumly, and, as of normal these days, pouted.

She hated feeling disappointed, one reason she generally didn't put herself out there. Her mind should be squarely focused on her work and on this campaign. Instead, she brooded like a teenager about Mr. Handsome Hatfield not showing up when he said he would. Between the angst over John and thoughts of the toll this campaign had taken on her business, Val felt downright wretched by the time the lights dimmed, signaling the audience to take their seats.

In the second half of the debate, Brown pulled random audience questions out of a bowl. As she asked the first one, Val held her breath. This could be a turning point in the event. Audience questions were unpredictable and their content would reveal something about the makeup of the crowd. A pro-Barton audience might ask questions aimed at derailing Gwen, and although Val believed in Gwen's ability to answer, she feared the personal attacks which would be part of this process. Sure enough, the first question was aimed at Gwen.

"Ms. Marsh, this constituent asks, 'You are far too young to hold the position of Mayor. How can we trust you to do the job well?'"

Val sighed. *What a ridiculous question. They should really go through these before they ask them.*

Gwen didn't even flinch. "Well, I'm not sure I would agree I'm too young. Cambria's charter defines the minimum age for this position as twenty-five, and I can assure you, that ship sailed a long time ago." A chuckle rose from the audience and an energized Gwen continued, "I hope you'll consider my work in the last four years on the council, as well as the countless hours I've spent on civic matters over the past seven years as evidence I'm not only trustworthy but making Cambria an amazing place to live has always been and will continue to be my focus." Generous applause followed, and Val relaxed a bit.

"The next question is for Mayor Barton. This constituent asks, 'Mayor Barton, some of your actions in this campaign could be seen as political bullying and an abuse of power. Do you think it is appropriate for a candidate to win political support through force and coercion?'"

It was eerily close to Val's question. Others had taken note of Barton's increasingly outrageous behavior during the campaign.

Barton cleared his throat and assumed the most sinister-looking smile Val had ever seen. "Must not be my biggest fan," he chuckled, and the audience followed suit. A wave of disgust crept over Val as Barton pulled out his good guy act. She wanted nothing more than to go home.

"You folks know me," Barton said. "I want to continue serving Cambria as I have for the past four years." The crowd burst into applause. *What a horrible answer!*

The debate continued in the same vein. No matter how precisely Gwen answered a question or how engaged the audience seemed to be, Barton made them cheer louder, every time, regardless of how empty and ridiculous his answers were. Val supposed she shouldn't be surprised – the audience consisted largely of Barton supporters, and, honestly, she couldn't imagine what Gwen could have done better. Her cousin handled every question about her age and appearance with grace and charm, even though Val found them degrading. She'd had the audience laughing with her more than once. Barton seemed to stay one step ahead of her the entire evening, and by the time the debate ended, Val felt thoroughly discouraged.

Gwen, on the other hand, seemed ready to get on to the next step. At first, Val wondered if her cousin comprehended how badly the night had gone, but Gwen seemed to look at it as a move in the right direction. "At least they didn't boo me off the stage," she chuckled, "I mean, Agatha certainly raised the war cry right off the bat, didn't she?"

They debriefed on their way to their favorite all-night pancake shop and didn't stop as they crammed their faces full of delicious food. Neither had eaten dinner, and the pancakes and coffee revived them. Nevertheless, Val wore an expression that betrayed her level of stress and anxiety.

"It's par for the course, Val," Gwen said between bites. "A debate hosted by the Republican Women would never be a Gwen-fest and, quite frankly, I'm happy it didn't turn into a slaughter. The City Clerk's debate next week is the real thing – televised and held at Thompson Auditorium on campus. Last election, they filled the place. Almost two thousand people in person and another ten thousand watching." She guzzled down some coffee.

While the pancakes had certainly helped the overall mood of the evening, Val remained pretty raw. John had never showed up, and when she texted him, she'd gotten no response.

She shoved her silent phone way down in her purse to prevent the temptation to check it every two seconds. And despite Gwen's enthusiasm and reassurance, the debate had left Val feeling more disenchanted with the whole political scene than ever.

"Gwen, look, I know what you're saying is true, and I love you so much, but I don't think I want to do this anymore," Val finally managed to say, knowing Gwen wouldn't accept this decision without a fight.

Gwen barely flinched. "You just need some sleep. You'll feel better tomorrow." Gwen chewed a few more bites of pancake, caught up in her own thoughts.

For whatever reason, her cousin's casual dismissal finally pushed Val over the edge. She didn't want to have her fears discounted so quickly. Feeling somewhat childish, but unable to stop herself, Val slid out of the booth, flung a ten-dollar bill dramatically on the table and said, "I'm done, Gwen."

Before Gwen could even protest, Val turned and walked out the door, called a cab, and went home. By the time she set her purse down, it buzzed constantly. Three missed calls and about a dozen texts from Gwen. Val turned off the ringer, threw her phone back in her purse, and went to bed. She was exhausted and angry, more with herself than anyone. She wasn't proud of her behavior with Gwen, and the more she thought about it, the more disgusted she felt. So, instead of thinking about it, she pulled her covers over her head and lay still until she finally fell asleep.

* * *

Val woke feeling like a first-class idiot. She'd thrown a tantrum and, although ashamed, she wasn't the least interested in facing the music. She decided to work from home, still in full avoidance mode, in hopes that hiding out would make all her problems disappear. She fished her phone out of her purse. Another dozen texts from Gwen and also one from John. She opened his message. *I'm so sorry for missing the debate! We had a water leak at the plant, and I forgot my phone on my desk. What a disaster! Can I see you today?*

Even hearing from John didn't ease her sense of dread. Instead of answering his text, she simply put her phone aside and continued to ignore it, though it made her feel even more like a jerk. A shower, cup of coffee, and piece of toast later, Val decided to go back to bed. She slept most of the day, and every time she thought about getting up, she told herself she deserved a day off and rolled back over. Around three in the afternoon, she moved the pity party to the couch.

With nothing but self-imposed free time on her hands, Val's mind wandered into painful territory. She wondered if her dad felt this way in the days after his business failed. Val's mother had complained he spent too much time sleeping. Too many days he didn't get out of bed or wouldn't get dressed and leave the house for any reason. Val had begun to see her father had suffered from something far more consuming than a broken heart, and it caused her to rethink her life in ways neither comfortable nor welcome. She feared following in her father's footsteps, and finally decided that understanding the situation better, opening herself to the truth, was the only way to ensure that wouldn't happen.

Val's usual operation didn't involve facing fears head-on. Reluctantly, she called her mother. The dutiful daughter, Val had called every other weekend since her mother had moved across the country. Besides those calls, she couldn't remember the last time she'd reached out. Now, as she dialed, guilt and shame mixed with fear and anxiety over how the conversation might go overwhelmed Val. Her mother picked up on the second ring.

"Valerie?" Her mother was the only person in the world who insisted on calling her by her full name. "Is everything okay?" Her mother's voice sounded overly cautious, guarded. Val never called out-of-the-blue.

"I don't know, Mom. Honestly, I'm having a hard time dealing with life right now, and I think maybe I need to talk about Dad." Val's mom sighed loudly. In the past, Val had insisted they never speak of her father.

"Gwen called this morning," her mother said.

"I need to call her and apologize. She's probably furious with me," Val said.

"She's not mad, honey. She's worried. I think she always worries you might suffer from depression, too."

The words struck a chord with Val. She'd gotten so used to thinking about her father's death in terms of a broken heart that she'd almost completely stopped thinking of his depression as possibly a real and treatable mental health disorder. She'd avoided thinking about serious things like this for so long it hadn't even occurred to her how her behavior might be perceived by other people, especially Gwen.

"Mom, please tell me about Dad. I mean everything, especially how bad it got at the end."

Val listened intently as her mother told her about her father's depression. Val was surprised to hear he'd actually been formally diagnosed by a psychiatrist, and he'd been on medication to treat his depression long before his business failed.

"I can't believe I never knew that. We talked so often. How did I miss it?" Val said, seeking absolution.

"Your father was extremely private about his feelings, even with me, and he never wanted anyone to worry about him. That hurt me the most, because no matter what he did, it affected me and our whole family. No matter how much he tried to hide his pain, I knew it was there. He closed me out so completely I felt powerless." Her mother's voice cracked, and for the first time since her father's death, Val allowed herself to truly acknowledge her mother's long suffering.

Val saw for the first time how much she resembled her father. She'd carefully constructed a wall between herself and other people, even those she loved most. She'd hardly spoken to her mother and sister over the years. She'd selfishly held her grief close to her, unwilling to see they'd been grieving, too. She'd used her father as a crutch, as a reason to avoid taking risks, to avoid anything uncomfortable or unpleasant.

"Mom, I'm so sorry," Val said, and for the first time, they cried together. They mourned her father and their lost years. They spent another hour on the phone, talking and crying and laughing and sharing.

Val hung up completely drained. She texted Gwen a quick *I'm sorry and I'm ok* message. John had texted twice more during the day, his messages sounding somewhat frantic. She texted him back. *Taking a mental health day. Will touch base tomorrow.*

Her stomach rumbled. She realized she hadn't eaten since breakfast and decided to order a pizza. When it arrived, she gobbled down as many slices as she could, put on a romantic comedy, and spent the rest of the evening dozing and trying to figure out what to do next.

CHAPTER 10

When Val woke on Thursday morning, she still reeled from her emotional day. Her mom had sent her an *I love you* text, and she smiled, knowing things could be different for them from this point on. Now she needed to decide what to do about Gwen.

She still didn't feel terribly motivated to go back to the campaign, despite a growing determination to change her outlook. She was uncomfortably vulnerable, and hadn't figured out exactly what to do. She finally understood her father's depression had played a major role in his decline, both personally and professionally, but she couldn't ignore the fact that Barton's threats were having a tangible effect on her business, her livelihood. Did she want to accept the consequences of seeing this campaign through to its conclusion? She didn't know for sure.

She picked up her phone and sifted through the messages from Gwen. Most were short, asking for a call back or checking in. A few were longer – messages imploring her to reconsider, reassuring her, making promises. The most recent texts sounded desperate, and though she hated to admit it, Val was kind of surprised at having aroused those feelings in Gwen. She dialed Gwen but got her voicemail. Val left a message saying she would be taking another day off to think about things, and she still didn't know if she wanted to work on the campaign.

She knew Gwen wanted to hear something different, but she couldn't honestly commit herself to anything more.

Finally, Val sent John a message. *Taking another day off. Will text you later.*

She needed to think about how John fit into her life. Her cautious nature made her wonder whether she could even fall in love with someone she'd only met a few weeks ago. She doubted. She agonized. And above all, she imagined the worst. Honestly, she was scared to death of the intensity of their relationship. It wasn't in her nature to picture a happy ending, though she hoped to have one someday. She imagined how completely broken she would feel if she loved and lost him.

Her phone buzzed. *I miss you.*

She smiled but didn't respond. A relationship with John Hatfield involved having her picture taken and posted on the Internet without her permission. Being the center of so much gossip and whispered conversations when they were out together had become hard to ignore.

She was never at ease with John. On one hand, he made her feel joyful and alive. On the other, he made her feel anxious, her emotions on a perpetual roller coaster with breathtaking highs and lows that scared her. Her overblown reactions during the debate made her feel relieved to have another day without seeing him.

Val preferred when things were tranquil, level. She kept her life deliberately on an even keel, avoiding anything too extreme in either direction. Until now, she'd never stopped to wonder how many amazing experiences she'd missed because of this philosophy.

Ugh. The whole situation frustrated her. Left to her own devices, Val could think herself in circles. Keeping busy with work helped her avoid this confusing spiral. She logged onto her computer and started tackling everyday tasks. After a few hours, her life seemed almost normal.

Gwen stayed noticeably quiet, as had John. In fact, Val's phone didn't buzz all morning or into the afternoon, giving her much-needed breather. Around four, she got a dinner invite from Gwen but decided to pass, not ready for the inevitable sales pitch. She settled in for another quiet night at home, putting together a tasty stir-fry and deciding on another chick flick to pass the time.

She'd finished dinner and gotten about ten minutes into the movie, when her doorbell rang. The sound startled her. She never had uninvited guests and deliveries were left downstairs.

"Who is it?' she called, wishing she had a peephole.

"John."

A rush of adrenaline shot through her, excitement at the prospect of seeing John and a twinge of irritation he'd come without even texting her first. She opened the door and invited him in.

He leaned down to peck her on the cheek, but didn't linger, instead moving into the apartment's interior and waiting politely to be offered a seat. His expression looked cold, reserved, and it made her instantly nervous. Without thinking, she resigned herself to being dumped despite not officially having a relationship.

"Do you feel better?" he asked, hesitantly, his face still blank.

"Yes. I had a pretty horrible Tuesday night and needed to take a break from everything," she said, hoping the explanation would satisfy him but knowing it wouldn't. He remained still, his face frozen somewhere between serious and brooding.

"Gwen called this morning asking about you," he said. She was a taken aback to hear her cousin had contacted him, but then again, Val had pretty much cut her off, too. "I told her I hadn't seen you. She seemed surprised to hear that."

"I'm sorry she bothered you," Val said, possibly one of the most pathetic responses she could have come up with. The atmosphere in the room was icy and the conversation strained.

"I don't mind that she called me, Val," he said, the tension in his voice rising. "I'm really stressed that you've been so distant.

I've spent the past two days kicking myself for not calling you Tuesday night and coming over here right away. And honestly, I'm frustrated that you're shutting me out." John heaved a huge sigh of relief as the words spilled out – he'd obviously been holding them in.

Sensing the emotional danger of the situation, Val went on the defensive. "You know, John, we're not exactly a couple. We've only known each other for a few weeks. We've only been on a couple of dates!" The sting of her words seemed to minimize the intimacy they'd shared, and Val wished she'd never said them. She had overreacted and spiraled out of control. John looked like she'd slapped him, but he recovered quickly and lashed out.

"I'm sorry, Val, I thought we had actually started something here." Bruised and bristling, staying mad to avoid feeling hurt, John rarely found himself in a position where he couldn't charm his way through. His chest ached. He'd never imagined feelings could be so physically painful. He felt powerless to get things back on track with Val.

"Look," she practically spat. "My life was completely calm and quiet before you decided to take it over." She fumed, though she experienced more terror than anger. She practically screamed at the man she'd fallen in love with. In her current mental state, she should have avoided this kind of conversation.

"I get that about you, Val. I'm not exactly comfortable with this, either. I was pretty happy with my life before you. If you don't want to see me, fine, but don't shut me out. Just tell me, dammit! Be honest with me!" His voice cracked, his control failed. His eyes looked desperate and full of feeling as he turned to face her. "Just tell me," he said weakly, his shoulders sagged, his voice barely a whisper.

Val's raging emotions dissipated, and she looked into John's eyes, seeing his confusion and frustration. She wanted to hold him and apologize, but fear prevented her. Instead, she said, coolly, "I think you should go. This isn't working." She turned away as her eyes welled with tears. She resented the tears, the blushing, all the things in her face that gave her emotions away. She was weak and exhausted.

John stood to face her. "Stop being so afraid, Val! You're an amazing woman. There's no reason to hide from life like this!" He was exasperated and at a loss for what to do next.

John walked past Val toward the door, his arm brushing hers, causing her to inhale quickly like she'd been shocked. The sound caused him to pause. He turned and looked into her eyes. He saw the tears, the rage, the fear. All his anger and hurt melted away, and he realized that more than anything, he wanted to comfort her.

He froze. It occurred to him that if he left now, he might never see her again. The thought of losing the broken woman standing before him was too much. His heart ached, and where his feelings had been muddled and undecided, he now had sudden clarity.

Instinctively, he moved toward Val, wrapped his arms around her, pulled her to him, breathing in the smell of her hair. Her body, which had been stiff and tense, relaxed into his embrace. He could feel her sigh as she wrapped her arms around him. He bent down to kiss her, and his lips crashed into hers with such force, with such intensity, that it left her breathless. She kissed him back, relishing the softness and the urgency in his lips.

His hands slipped into her hair, caressing the back of her neck, brushing her hair back as his mouth moved down under her ear and toward her shoulder. She tilted her head slightly and moaned as warmth flooded her body. His hands moved down her back, keeping her close as he continued to brush his lips along her neck and over her cheeks, her eyes, her forehead.

She pushed his jacket off his shoulders, and it fell onto the floor behind him. She ran her hands over his chest and up to his face, cupping his cheeks in her hands and kissing him passionately. He slid his hands down to her waist and then up into her shirt, passing his warm hands over her bare skin with fervor, memorizing every curve, tracing her spine, feeling her body respond to his touch.

Keeping him close, she backed slowly down the hall into her bedroom, falling gently onto the bed and pulling him slowly onto her. His lips moved down her neck, over her throat, his touches leaving a trail of fiery sensation. All the while, his hands caressed every inch of her flesh. He pushed her shirt up over her head, catching her arms above her as he kissed the skin between her breasts and down toward her stomach. Any self-consciousness she might have had evaporated. His touches were greedy. She could feel his desire, a palpable wave of emotion and need washing over her. She wanted John more than she'd ever wanted another man.

"John?" She whispered when their lips parted, but he covered her mouth in another kiss. Little by little, they removed the rest of their clothing, unnecessary obstacles to their connection. The skin on his chest smoldered hot against hers, and as he moved his hands down her sides and over her hips. She moved into him, pressing herself hard into his body. His desire for her made him feel crazy. They were lost in each other, and for the next few hours, they explored one another, never speaking a word, using their fingers and tongues to memorize every detail, eliciting sounds of pleasure, hot breath rolling off their skin.

The closeness was unlike anything Val had ever experienced before, and the sex was profound, delicious, more intense than she could have imagined. Later, her memory of the night became a mix of reality and fantasy, actual and imagined details indistinguishable from one another. During and after, scenes flashed through her mind, both increasing her need for him and blurring her thoughts so that she finally stopped trying to sort things out and gave herself over to her physical being.

His arms wrapped around her. He draped his leg over hers,

exploring her curves and the softness of her breasts. John rolled onto his back, pulling her on top of him, resting his hands on her hips as they moved in rhythm. His hands moving with confidence between her legs, his fingers causing electricity to fill her abdomen, warmth spreading down her legs and throughout her body.

When their lovemaking ended, they wrapped themselves tightly together, pulled the covers over their heads, and refused to budge for what seemed like a blissful eternity. They dozed. Val rested her head on John's chest, feeling his breathing and letting his calming heartbeat lull her to sleep. When she awoke, he ran his hands gently through her hair. It was still dark outside though Val felt refreshed, awake, and happy.

"Hi," she said, sleepily, enjoying the feel of his hands in her hair.

"Hi back," he said, his voice husky and warm. "I'm sorry I woke you."

Unwilling to move her head from his chest, Val smiled and stroked his chest and stomach, letting her fingers wander the path down his navel. His body stiffened slightly as she moved lower and her smile broadened.

"What time is it?" she asked.

"It's almost five," he said, his hands moving down over her back, soothing and warm. Then, he said softly, "I'm sorry ..." There was a hint of sadness in his voice, and it brought Val out of her reverie. She leaned up on her elbow and looked into his eyes. They brooded and she was puzzled. A sense of foreboding took over and she got cold.

"What is it? What's wrong?" She tried to sound calm, but her voice betrayed her sudden tension.

"I'm sorry for butting in here last night," he said, looking serious. "I was going crazy with worry, and when Gwen called, I couldn't keep myself away."

Val sighed, feeling frustrated in what should have been

a blissful moment. Why did he worry? Was this regret? Always quick to jump to conclusions, Val stiffened and moved away from John, protecting herself, her heart, from whatever pain was on the horizon.

John's emotions ran high, barely under control. He'd woken up feeling blissful. And then, as he watched Val sleep, he'd begun worrying, concerned she'd wake up regretting their night together. He couldn't shake the feeling she might disappear at any moment. Up to this point, John had kept a safe distance from relationships, never allowing anyone in. With Val, he was lost in love. She was always on his mind, in his heart. It terrified him.

"Why are you backing away?" Irritation mounted, and he slipped off his edge of the bed and started pulling clothes on. In a flash, the morning slipped out of his control. He didn't know how to salvage it. He feared making himself any more vulnerable with Val. He berated himself for acting so badly, but he couldn't seem to stop.

"John, I'm sorry." Her voice was barely audible as she reached out for him. Her touch on his back stopped his muddled brain from bursting. He took in a slow breath and turned to face her.

"Val," he started, then paused. He wanted to say he loved her. And he wanted to run away, back to the safety of his apartment, his life, his work … all the things he knew and trusted. Instead, he said simply, "I should go home. I have to be to work in a few hours."

He finished dressing and prepared to leave. Val laid in bed, watching him, her eyes heavy with distress. He walked to her side of the bed and sat down. She curled her body around him instinctively. The contact made them both relax, and John smiled.

"We're both too stubborn to make this easy, aren't we?" He chuckled softly and leaned down to kiss her cheek. Staying close to her face, he whispered, "I *will* see you later today." And he left.

CHAPTER 11

After John left, Val went back to sleep. When she awoke again, it was in a haze of love and confusion. She lay in bed for as long as she could, holding on to the feeling of John beside her. His departure had been stressful and frustrating, though it made her realize this relationship seemed as hard on him as on her. Being together was both easy and difficult. She couldn't picture anyone she'd ever felt more herself with, but she felt positively idiotic around him as well. So perplexing!

Reluctantly, she got out of bed. After showering, Val dressed and headed to her office. As she walked, the intensity of the night came back in waves, and as she stopped for breakfast and neared her office, she tried to regain some sense of normalcy. But it proved elusive. There was nothing *normal* about her life now. Everything had changed.

She thought back to when John had shown up at her door, looking all disappointment and despair. She'd assumed things were over. The night had taken an unexpected turn, and now she was more confused than ever, so far out of her comfort zone she didn't know how to get back, or if she even wanted to. She could no longer deny her love for John, and she believed he loved her back. So, why the confusion? Shouldn't she be overcome with happiness?

Why must you make everything so difficult, she said to herself, exasperated. Val sighed and said the words, "I want this!" to herself like a mantra. The more she said it, the more she realized how true it was.

She found it nearly impossible to concentrate work at the office. She logged into her computer, but after half an hour of staring at the screen, she realized she would have to move to keep herself grounded. She called Gwen and asked to meet for lunch. Gwen's voice sounded full of both relief and irritation. Honestly, Val couldn't blame her. These last two days had given Val some much needed time for introspection, but her cousin, in the midst of a contentious campaign, couldn't slow down until the election. Val knew her cousin relied on her, and her disappearance probably made Gwen a nervous wreck.

Val spent the next few hours considering the campaign and her role in it. She started with a pro and con list about sticking with Gwen, trying to arrive at a well-thought out and logically supported reason to stay out of it. Her list didn't cooperate. The more Val thought about the campaign and Barton and the whole messy situation, the decision to stay on board and see it through hardened in her mind. Something had happened to Val. Facing the truth about her father's depression had made it impossible for her to hide behind her fear entirely, and a new seed of anger and indignation at Barton's behavior took root.

At eleven-thirty, Val put on her coat and walked into the sunny fall day to meet with Gwen at their favorite Mediterranean restaurant a few blocks away. The cool crisp air hit her face, reviving her, making her feel a new sense of clarity. After almost a decade running her business, Val believed she could take control of her destiny and endure the risks. When she met Gwen at the door, her cousin gave her a quizzical look.

"Everything alright?" Gwen asked with a peculiar expression on her face. "You look … different. Happy even."

Val laughed and grabbed Gwen's hand to give it a squeeze. "I am happy, as it turns out."

They walked inside and took a table toward the back where

they could talk. Val gobbled down her chicken pita wrap like she hadn't eaten in a week. Gwen nibbled at her gyro and examined Val, trying to figure out what exactly had happened without having to ask.

"I guess your mental health days did the trick, eh?" Gwen asked, flatly.

"Yes. And Gwen, I'm so sorry for walking out on you the other night." Val searched her cousin's face for a reaction, but Gwen maintained her guard. "I'm figuring out a few things about myself, and I think I used my fears about this campaign as an excuse. In fact, I'm sure I've made excuses for a long time." Val wasn't quite sure where to go from there.

"Val, I knew when I asked you to work on the campaign with me that you were never been comfortable in the spotlight, and I knew you'd end up in a tight spot now and then." Gwen took a deep breath and continued. "It was selfish of me to ask you to do this, and I want you to know I'm fine with you walking away from the campaign. But not from me, okay?"

Val was overcome. She and Gwen had always been like sisters. Best friends. And in all their adult years, she'd never seen Gwen quite as fearful as she was now. Empathy flooded Val's system, and she reached out to take Gwen's hand again, this time knowing exactly what she needed to say.

"Gwennie. I love you. Forever. I would never let anything, including this campaign, get between us. I never meant to worry you." She paused briefly. "And I think, if you'll let me, I'd like to see this campaign through to the end."

Finally, Gwen's expression changed, this time to one of shock. She clearly hadn't expected that answer.

"Are you sure?" she asked, giving Val a moment to come to her senses, but the smile on Val's face never budged for a moment.

"Very sure," Val said. "I'm one hundred percent confused about practically everything else, but I've got this part figured out, at least."

"All right, so what's the sudden revelation all about?" Gwen asked, her curiosity piqued.

Val's face betrayed her immediately. Her cheeks flushed, and she conjured the most ridiculous grin that had ever graced a face.

Gwen practically squealed, "John?"

Val nodded, "He came over last night to talk some sense into me," she giggled. "We got into a fight and ended up in bed."

Gwen's jaw dropped to the floor. "And?"

"And, I'm in love," Val said simply and happily, and with sudden confidence. "With John Hatfield, and it's the scariest feeling ever!"

Her heart raced as she spoke. She painted a surface-level sketch of the night with John's intrusion into her space and ending with the weirdness of the morning, skipping most of the juicy details, which she held onto tightly, unwilling to reveal, as if speaking them aloud might take away a bit of the magic.

"Good grief, you two will drive each other crazy," Gwen chuckled. "And the rest of us, too!" She looked genuinely happy, and Val was so relieved to share this secret with her best friend.

But work awaited. Without another moment's hesitation, Val said, "Enough mushy talk. We have to get back to work, right?"

They spent the rest of lunch and most of the afternoon in Val's office strategizing. Three weeks remained until the election, and every moment counted – press, advertising, social media blitzes, appearances, debates, and a push to get early voting underway. In Colorado, voters receive their ballots via mail, so it wasn't surprising that most candidates became focused on getting them mailed back in as the election neared.

With 127,000 registered voters in Cambria and high turn-out, going door-to-door to speak with voters took top priority for any candidate with a realistic chance of winning. Gwen had started the campaign out with a small but loyal legion of supporters. As the weeks had passed, her numbers climbed. Despite his so-called win in Tuesday's debate, Barton was losing ground. His base remained dedicated as ever, but undecided voters turned out in droves to support Gwen.

The City Clerk's debate loomed a week and a half away, so preparing for this debate became high on the list. Unlike the Republican Women's debate, audience questions would be collected before this next debate and only a handful chosen, representing a wider variety of topics, most of which would require an intimate understanding of city operations. Both Gwen and Barton had plenty of experience working with the city, so it seemed likely the clerk's office would choose more complicated questions to ferret out specific types of expertise. Preparation was key.

As the day neared its close, Val daydreamed again about John. Contemplation and hard work had settled Val more than she had been in weeks. So, when she hadn't heard from him by five, Val decided to text him. She heard back immediately, and within five minutes had dinner plans for the night. John showed up at her office around six, smiling. The tension of the morning had dissipated.

John's smile was infectious, and he and Val walked into *Il Fornaio*, an elegant and cozy Italian restaurant in downtown Cambria, with stupid grins plastered firmly on their faces. The hostess raised an eyebrow when she saw them walk in hand in hand. She clearly recognized John. Val didn't care. She could finally handle this relationship despite its inevitably public nature.

They sat at a cozy corner table. The waiter handed them their menus, lit a candle, and gave them a few minutes to decide what to order. Without even glancing at the menu, John reached across the table and took Val's hands, both of them relieved by the physical connection.

"I'm an idiot," John said, smiling warmly across at her. "Please forgive me for this morning's stupidity. I need to tell you two things right this second before I wimp out."

Val held her breath and tried not to look too ridiculous when she let out a mouthful of air and tried to breathe evenly.

"First, I am crazy in love with you, Val. I know we've only known each other a few weeks, but I know exactly how I feel about you, and there it is." He paused before he went on. "Second, I am scared shitless. I admit, I've never felt this way about anyone, and I'm terrified you'll disappear on me." He exhaled, shoulders heaving, and looked at her. His relief at having gotten that off his chest was palpable and Val smiled broadly, which seemed to give him courage.

"I know how you feel on both counts," she said. "I love you, too." Val squeezed his hand. Having the words out of her mouth made them feel so much more real, solid. It gave them shape, and they took on a life of their own. "I won't disappear again, I promise."

When the waiter returned, it was an awkward intrusion. John and Val sat, hands entwined, gazing at each other. Hoping to get rid of him quickly, they both ordered salads, lasagna, and a glass of wine. Then, settling in for a completely unhurried evening, they chatted about their respective days. Val recounted her afternoon with Gwen and their work on the campaign.

"I'm glad you decided to stick with the campaign," John said with a grin.

"I've always backed away from anything scary. I have to keep reminding myself this campaign can't kill me. I've gotten where I am through hard work and determination."

John wasn't sure if Val tried to convince him or herself but gladly accepted the change in her perspective.

"My day wasn't nearly so exciting," John chuckled, describing a typical day in the world of paper products. "And of course," he said, grinning sheepishly, "I spent a fair amount of time daydreaming."

"Me, too." The admission made her blush. For a few moments, they gazed at each other like lovesick teenagers.

Pretty sure their romantic meal had an observer, Val made accidental eye contact with someone from another table. Luckily, it didn't take long to let the attention fade into the background, and before the meal was done, Val found she truly didn't care whether people watched. She could immerse herself completely in John without worrying about everyone else. It was liberating.

John invited Val back to his apartment, and they cuddled on the couch, watching a movie. They made it through ten minutes before they retired to the bedroom for what turned out to be a perfect end to a perfect evening. They made love, this time slowly, gently, and in the morning there was nothing but happiness between them. John's bedroom looked out toward the mountains, and they watched the sun rise, wrapped in each other's arms, John's long legs draped over Val's.

Unlike their first night, silent and intense, now they talked, discussing every topic they could think of, soaking up the other's thoughts and words voraciously, learning and growing together. In the span of less than forty-eight hours, they'd gone from the unlikeliest couple to a unit, inseparable, unconquerable.

Val told John about the talk with her mother. She spoke honestly for the first time in her life about her father, admitting all her fears and misconceptions. She was vulnerable, and when the walls began to creep up, John would kiss her gently on the forehead or rub her back, and she relaxed into the moment. She trusted John.

When they finally couldn't ignore the time any longer, Val got dressed and John drove her home. He lingered at her door, kissing her tenderly, and with one final, "I love you," went to begin his day. Val had promised Gwen a day of work, and John was scheduled to fly to Seattle that evening for a meeting at their Pacific Northwest plant early Sunday morning. It would be a busy weekend for both, but they were secure in their newfound love and ready to take on the world.

* * *

Gwen came over at ten, and they worked for several hours before grabbing a late lunch and relocating to Gwen's house. Her campaign manager, Victoria, joined them, and the trio plotted the days leading up to the next debate. By dinnertime, the schedule was mainly settled. Each day leading up to the election would include a strategy meeting with Gwen's volunteer staff for canvassing instructions and check-in. Val would schedule press coverage and interviews for Gwen when possible. In the evenings, Gwen, Victoria, and Val would meet back at Gwen's house to discuss the day and make any changes to their plans.

Despite the rigorous schedule, Val actually looked forward to the work. She was in her zone, and when she found this sweet spot, she became a workaholic. Helping Gwen win the election had become as much a personal goal as a professional one.

Barton's campaign ads began to turn ugly. Opposing groups, like the Conservative Women Voters, called Gwen's credentials into question and spun her voting record to make her look downright wishy-washy. Trying to figure out when and where and whether to address these ads became a constant topic of conversation.

Saturday came and went. Sunday morning around ten, Val was still in bed, enjoying the only downtime she'd likely get over the next few weeks. John had texted earlier to say hello. He'd fly home later in the afternoon. Val had convinced herself that dealing with other client work today was smart given the distractions the campaign was likely to pose during the week. But she wouldn't budge until she had to.

An interesting development in election coverage happened online. In general, Jabber stayed equally critical of all candidates, scrutinizing, questioning, and taking pains to point out flaws and inconsistencies in each candidate. Lately, the website's tone had shifted decidedly pro-Gwen, and with over 100,000 site visits, there was something very exciting about the change in focus. Val had read the coverage for weeks, nodding in approval each time Barton got called on the carpet and bristling anytime Gwen's experience or youth were called into question.

The great thing about working for Gwen's campaign was Gwen herself. Honest and straightforward, Gwen worked hard to build a campaign truly aligned with the people rather than Cambria's special interests. Where Barton represented the voice of the conservative upper class, Gwen's approach to politics was more even. She stayed clear about her views and didn't deviate without good reason. Even in cases when she couldn't support the proverbial little guy she explained herself fully and in terms people could understand. Despite the relentless hours of the campaign, Gwen normally arrived first for council meetings and ended up the last to leave.

Right before dinner, Val pulled up Jabber and nearly had a heart attack when she saw the headline – *Mayor Barton Cited for Improper Use of Funds*. Val read with rapt attention as the site built the case against Barton with precision. He'd been cited by the Secretary of State for improper use of campaign funds for personal expenses. While the citation itself seemed minor and resulted in little more than a slap on the wrist, the website revealed Barton was also undergoing further scrutiny by the city's auditor for travel expenses related to official business. Val inhaled deeply, her pulse rising. If true, Barton could be facing professional reprimand, or worse.

Val texted Gwen. *Did you see Jabber?*

Gwen texted back immediately. *Yes. I bet Roger's furious.*

Need to consider a slight change in tactics.

Sure, boss. See you in the morning.

Val put down her phone and finished perusing local news sites, but they contained no other mention of possible allegations against Barton. Around seven, Val heated up some soup and waited. John had texted from the airport and would be with her soon. When he arrived, all thoughts of the campaign were put on hold. In fact, Val didn't mention the Jabber post until the following morning.

John not only wasn't surprised, he reacted to the news with a strange expression, smug and knowing. Before Val could ask more, John offered to make coffee and trotted away from the bed. She laid back happily, thinking about how her life had changed.

Val got out of bed and showered. When she entered the kitchen, she found pancakes and coffee and the man she loved sitting at the table waiting for her, pleased at his own performance. She laughed softly, leaned in to give him a quick kiss, and settled in for the most domestic morning she'd ever spent with a man.

They walked to Val's office, hand in hand, and he dropped her off with a kiss and headed back to his car.

CHAPTER 12

The audit news broke. Every local channel buzzed about Barton's alleged improper use of official funds. Reporters on conservative stations lambasted Jabber for overdramatizing the situation. They placed the anonymous blogger inside the Marsh camp, though no one had successfully identified the individual. Liberal stations had taken the story and run with it, expanding the scrutiny over Barton's travel expenses to include everything from embezzlement to claims of sexual harassment.

For the first few moments of the workday, Val stared in wonder as the Internet churned the story into a disfigured monster, only vaguely recognizable as Jabber's original allegations. She felt a little sorry for Barton, knowing he had no choice at this point but to go on the defensive. His campaign had already issued a statement denying any wrongdoing and scheduled a full press conference that afternoon.

From a public relations perspective, Val studied movement in the media closely. Gwen had campaigned for her council seat on a platform of governmental transparency and fiscal responsibility, despite her more liberal opinions on social issues. This scandal, handled correctly, could be pivotal for Gwen. Her record remained unblemished, and her lack of experience in the case actually served as a blessing. She simply hadn't been on the political scene long enough to encourage the type of scrutiny Barton now underwent.

On the other hand, Val knew the situation required caution and cool heads. Attacking Barton's performance in any way at this point could embolden his base. Waiting for Gwen to appear for their scheduled meeting, Val weighed their options. By the time Gwen knocked at her door, she felt comfortable, confident.

Gwen sank down in an office chair. "My phone has been ringing off the hook. I've avoided talking to the media, but they're asking for a statement. I hope you have a plan."

"Well, first I need you to tell me everything you know about the allegations."

"His travel records are being audited. It happens every year. This year it looks like he overspent on two out-of-state trips. It's not that unusual, to be honest. The finance department would normally issue a letter addressing the discrepancy and ask for repayment for any unsupported expenses." Gwen sounded weary. "Honestly, the media has completely overblown this, and from what I hear, Roger is seeing red."

"So, is there anything like this that could come out about *you*?" Val winced at having to ask.

"No," Gwen said with a sigh. "I've only done a handful of trips during my time on the council, and they were all in-state. Very low cost."

"I figured I'd better ask just to be on the safe side. I watched the news all morning, and they've gobbled up the Jabber story. I read the blog post yesterday, and I didn't read nearly as much into it. I mean, it seemed bad but not to the extent the media has taken."

Gwen nodded. "Thing is, the record's office is being flooded with information requests and calls for a full-scale investigation on Barton's financial activities. As a council member, I would normally be involved in an investigation of this nature, but, of course, I can't. This whole situation just got all kinds of complicated."

Val patted Gwen's arm kindly. "Well, luckily, all we need to do is prepare a statement and stick to the script. Actually, your status as an active councilwoman gives us an excellent shield from all this. We simply can't comment. Period."

On hearing this, Gwen perked up a bit. "Thank goodness," she groaned. "I can't stand Roger, but I have no desire to get involved in this kind of mucky battle with him three weeks before the election."

Val nodded in agreement. "I suggest you tell the media you can't get involved in any investigation into the allegations, and that you trust the city to follow through appropriately."

"Check," Gwen said.

"And I'm preparing news releases about your financial records. Until we see how Roger's press conference goes, I'm not submitting anything. I don't want them to see you as kicking him while he's down."

"Agreed."

"Let's go meet the volunteers and start canvassing."

* * *

The Gwen Marsh for Mayor headquarters was a tiny, freezing-cold storefront in a strip mall in one of Cambria's older neighborhoods. They spent so little time there Gwen hadn't bothered turning on the heat. With three weeks until the election, there didn't seem to be any point. Gwen had loaded several space heaters into her car, and by the time the volunteers arrived around noon, the place was nice and toasty.

A large map of Cambria was spread out on a table in the middle of the room with thick lines dividing the city into grids. Volunteers would go door to door, providing leaflets about Gwen's campaign and encouraging people to vote. Twice a week, they would offer voter sessions at headquarters for anyone who wanted extra information or wanted to speak to Gwen personally. Each day, the canvassers were assigned to a square on the map and off they went, into the cool fall weather.

The campaign office had a big flat screen television mounted on the wall. At two, Gwen switched it on so they could watch Barton's press conference.

A red-faced Barton stood impatiently behind his campaign manager, Todd Hammond. Todd stepped up to the microphone, greeted the press, and read a prepared statement. Barton's financial records were undergoing the standard annual audit, and any discrepancies would be cited and dealt with immediately by the mayor. Hammond emphasized the routineness of the audit. He hesitated before giving the stage to Barton.

Unlike his campaign manager, Barton appeared visibly agitated. Stepping to the microphone, Barton cleared his throat loudly. "As Todd so eloquently put it, it's been brought to my attention the city may not cover a few of my expenses, and I'll take responsibility for those. As I always do." His tone was defensive, and Val saw Todd tap Roger's elbow gently, cautioning his irate candidate to stop.

Barton continued, "Look, folks, you know me. I've always done what's right for Cambria, and I urge you to ignore Jabber's false accusations. Why does he blog anonymously?" Roger's face grew redder by the moment. Val winced, hoping he'd shut up and sit back down. He didn't. Barton's face looked like it would burst into flames.

"I tell you what, he'd better stay away from my campaign."

Todd was on his feet, standing next to Barton, nearly pushing him away from the microphone.

Todd leaned into the microphone and said simply, "As you can see, Mayor Barton is quite upset about his reputation being slandered. Thank you. We won't be taking any questions." And with that, he took his candidate firmly by the arm and whisked him away from a media disaster in the making.

Val was stunned, and judging from the look on Gwen's face, she wasn't alone. Barton was a loose cannon. His usually charismatic façade had completely vanished, and what remained was a good deal unsettling. Val watched as the man imploded before her eyes.

Val took a breath. "Okay, yeah, I think we'll focus on giving Roger some space. He seems to be doing more damage to his campaign than we ever could."

Gwen, still staring blankly at the screen, nodded. Gwen and Roger weren't even remotely friendly, but having worked closely with him for the past four years, his demeanor flabbergasted her. He could act like an asshole, but right now he acted like an angry, out-of-control asshole.

Seeing the alarm on Gwen's face, Val said, "He's a control freak and a bully, Gwen. He's used to getting his way, and this campaign's not going his way."

"I'm really startled," said Gwen. "When we work for the city, we all have our roles to play. I guess I've been lucky to have the buffer of the council."

"When you insist on being horrible to everyone around you, eventually it's going to come back and bite you." Val's sympathy for Barton quickly vanished. She started thinking about the damage he'd already inflicted on her and John's businesses, and it didn't take long for contempt to build again.

"We have work to do, Gwen," Val said resolutely as she turned off the TV.

* * *

A little after five, canvassers started to return and report their successes. Gwen had turned on the evening news and smiled ear to ear as she watched the day's polling. She and Roger were now dead even. Gwen had gone from having only the most remote chances of winning to an attainable goal.

With everyone checked out for the night, Val and Gwen were packing up their things and getting ready to leave for the night when John walked in. Val's face lit up, and Gwen laughed to see her cousin so goofy in love. John hugged Val like he hadn't seen her in days.

"Looks like I'm going home alone, eh?" Gwen winked at Val.

"Actually," John interjected, "would you like to join us for dinner? I mean, assuming you want to have dinner tonight, Val?" He looked for approval from Val.

She smiled. Her reclusive boyfriend had started to act like a regular social animal.

"You don't mind, Val?" Gwen said, flattered by the invitation.

"Of course not." She turned to John. "Let's go to the Taphouse. I want to tell you about this weird day without being completely eavesdropped on."

Taking separate cars, they met up at the Taphouse, a popular and noisy place out on the highway. Its claim to fame was the best beer in town. Val didn't care for beer, but she thought they had a great French onion soup. And the booths had high walls which made it possible to have a quiet conversation over the rowdy din of the bar. It was the perfect place to gossip.

They chitchatted as they ordered drinks. John had checked in at the office and then spent the afternoon with his mother. Anne was on the planning committee for the annual Christmas charity dance hosted by the Women's Guild, and John had served as her date ever since his father passed away. John eventually started helping with the planning as well.

"This year's party is going to be something," John said, giving the girls a rundown on the plans. "My mother's a woman possessed. I've never seen her like this."

"Maybe she's excited you'll have a real date this year," Gwen suggested with a devilish grin. John blushed, and Val chuckled.

"You said it, not me." Val gave John a playful nudge, amused to not be the only target of Gwen's ribbing for once.

When the food arrived, the conversation got more serious. Gwen and Val recounted their day. John had watched the press conference with his mother.

"Mom has never been Barton's biggest fan, but she was concerned by how visibly upset he looked. She's known him and his wife for years. I think she's going to call Kathy to check in." John seemed unfazed by Barton's actions. "I think he's finally showing his true colors."

John told Gwen the details of Barton's angry visit to his office. Gwen looked worried. She looked at Val thoughtfully and then said, "You know, John, you might not want to make enemies with Roger. He may be a hothead but he's powerful, and this change in his public face definitely has me concerned."

John cleared his throat and shifted uncomfortably. "Yes, well, I may be partially responsible."

Val raised an eyebrow in John's direction. She knew he despised Barton, but she couldn't imagine he would intentionally provoke him.

"I have a confession to make, and you have to promise to keep it quiet," John continued. He winced as he said, "I know who the Jabber blogger is. I think I'm the only person who does. And I may have possibly helped him put together the story about the audits." John's face oozed guilt like a child who'd been caught with his hand in the cookie jar.

"You what?" Val said, confused. Then, as reality began to sink in, she thought about how favorably Jabber had been reporting on Gwen's campaign lately, and it started to make sense. "Wait, you're saying you've been feeding information to Jabber?"

"Are you serious?" Gwen asked. She was normally pretty good about keeping a cool head, but her expression betrayed her shock.

"I've been in cahoots with Jabber for the past four years. It started as a way of informing the public. I got disgusted during the last election by the lack of good, solid, understandable information, not to mention the blatant lies. When Jabber starting tackling the local political scene, I thought it might actually help fix the problem." John took a big swallow of beer and a larger gulp of air before continuing. He looked hard at Val, trying to read her expressions. "No one can know who the blogger is."

"Understandable," Val said, distractedly. Her mind raced, and her emotions careened all over the place. She hated surprises, and John's news was a bit shocking. Just when she'd gotten used to her personal space being invaded by dating a local celebrity, it turned out the local celebrity was also a spy.

"Val? Are you all right?" Gwen said, having turned her attention to her cousin when she spoke. Val's face had turned ashen.

"I'm fine. Just shocked." She looked at John, wondering why it seemed like her boyfriend had an alter ego. It felt strange to think about his involvement in something so public and mysterious. Her every move being viewed under a microscope, open to public consumption.

Gwen turned back to John. "How did you find out about the travel audit?"

"I've been following local politics for years. It seemed like luck more than anything that we stumbled on the discrepancies. Or maybe not luck, because I didn't realize the media would blow it so completely out of proportion." John looked guilty. "Don't get me wrong. I think Roger needs to answer for his actions," and he looked at Gwen, "but I would say the same thing about you, too, Gwen, if it ever came up."

Gwen chuckled, and the sound shook Val out of her trance.

"See, this is my whole point about transparency," Gwen said, with a self-satisfied tone. "If you keep everything out in the open, knuckleheads like you will have nothing to find."

John heaved a huge sigh of relief. He'd been worried about Gwen's reaction to his work with Jabber and, given his feelings for Val, he couldn't stand the thought of Gwen not liking him.

Val still looked somewhat shaken. John put his arm around her, and she relaxed a little. "Guess I'm going to have to be careful what I tell you now," she smiled weakly.

Looking her straight in the eyes, John said, his voice tight and serious. "I would never betray your trust, Val. Never." He touched her face and kissed her lightly on the cheek.

"Sorry. I've never been good with surprises." Val smiled warmly at him, but weariness grew inside of her. With all the changes going on in her life these days, her confidence was still shaky.

They talked about their lives the rest of the evening. John found himself liking Gwen. She and Val seemed as close as sisters. By the end of the evening, he and Gwen acted like old friends.

Val reflected on her sudden contentment. A few days ago, she'd been ready to hide away forever, and then something changed. Was it all about John? She didn't think so. Something in her perspective had changed. She embraced life more fully.

John walked Val to her car, held her tightly, and kissed her passionately.

Val giggled, running her hands through his hair and enjoying the nearness of his body. She'd been resolved to go back home and get a good night's sleep, alone. Now, not so resolved. They headed to her apartment, and the good night's sleep happened on the heels of love and passion.

In the early morning, John woke her up with soft kisses on the back of her neck. Val smiled, savoring the sensation.

"Good morning," she whispered.

"Good morning." His warm, soft voice in her ear sent a chill down her spine. She wanted to wake up to his voice every morning.

John wrapped his arms around Val, and without another word they drifted back to sleep, skin to skin, warm, content.

CHAPTER 13

Barton was conspicuously absent from the news over the next few days. Whether his handlers had banned him from any public appearances or he'd finally come to his senses, he was nowhere to be seen. Slowly, as the night of the debate approached, the financial scandal lost steam. The news sites moved on to other topics and things calmed down. Gwen's numbers continued to rise steadily. The canvassing team met with a mostly positive reception. Things went great, and Val felt comfortable about the pace of the campaign.

John had spent every night with her at her apartment, and waking up beside him each morning thrilled her. Val had spoken with her mother several times. The brief talks signaled a change in their relationship, and she was grateful. Val had taken the time to call a therapist and make an appointment. She now understood the countless unresolved feelings about her father and her family, and she was finally at a place in her life, loved and supported, where she wanted to deal with those problems head-on.

The debate, scheduled for Friday night, took place each mayoral election year at the university's main auditorium in front of a packed audience. For only the second time, the debate would be broadcast live on all three local television stations. Gwen's energy level increased throughout the week while Val worked hard to maintain a calm demeanor. John's quiet presence kept her tendency to overdramatize in check, but she still found herself overreacting a bit. She got caught up in the details and found herself stressed about even the most insignificant things.

She spent more than the usual amount of time leading up to the debate preparing questions and answers with Gwen. Luckily, her cousin's campaign had been encouraging constituents to provide questions and feedback since day one. Gwen's insistence on taking time to personally answer each question had been incredibly effective, and the questions had poured in. With a few hours to spare before they headed over to the auditorium, Gwen and Val parked themselves at their favorite diner for a good dose of sustenance.

"You ready?" Val said between ravenous bites of burger and fries. The week had taken its toll, and she was ready for a few days off.

"Yep. I'm feeling great, actually," Gwen said, smiling. "Hungry, though. Glad we decided to eat before show time this week."

"Me, too," said Val, wondering how big a part hypoglycemia had played in the previous week's post-debate freak-out. *Oh well, I wouldn't trade last week for anything,* she thought to herself.

"I'm curious how Roger's going to do tonight," Gwen noted. As much as she loved a good debate, there was apprehension going into this evening's event. She didn't want to get dragged into the muck with Barton, and his anger, barely contained these days, concerned her.

"Hopefully, he'll demonstrate his usual horrible self," Val said. She tried to strike a jesting tone, but she had the same behavioral concerns about Barton as her cousin. She was much more comfortable with his predictable condescension than with his angry outbursts.

When they arrived at the auditorium, it buzzed with frantic energy. The event crew busily prepared the stage and performed sound checks. A VIP seating section had been set up in front of the stage. Val knew the governor and Constance would attend. Val planned on snagging a seat next to Constance, hoping a friendly face would keep her nerves in check.

John showed up early to wish Gwen luck and then took a seat in the stands. Val found John in a tight huddle with a blond guy who looked familiar. She knew she'd seen him somewhere before, but she couldn't place him.

For someone who spent almost no time on the social scene, John was in-tune with what went on in Cambria's politics and had turned into quite an asset on behalf of Gwen's campaign. His offers to contribute financially were refused politely. Now that Val and John dated, Gwen was cautious about managing their reputations, aware that any hint of impropriety could damage Val's business and maybe even Gwen's campaign. Luckily, Gwen had acclimated to campaigning on a shoestring. What she lacked in advertising power, she made up for in true civic engagement. And John's insights were far more valuable than any monetary donation.

The candidates were asked to arrive at least a half an hour before start time. Barton and his wife walked in with about three minutes to spare. He escorted his wife to a seat in the VIP section, and made his way toward the stage where Gwen and the moderator, local news anchor Kent Travis, engaged in friendly banter.

The mood changed when Barton joined them. He greeted Kent coolly and barely acknowledged Gwen at all. Kent jumped right into the format for the debate, pointing out where the timekeeper would be seated and discussing the ground rules.

Governor and Mrs. Carlton arrived about ten minutes later, and Val was relieved to see Constance. They took seats in the VIP front row and watched the crowds roll in. The rest of the section soon filled with councilmen and their spouses, members of the university administration, and the Attorney General, who happened to be in town for another event. The governor and the A.G. chatted amiably. Constance and Val kept close watch on the exchanges taking place near the stage.

"Roger looks awful, as usual," Constance whispered to Val.

"It's hard to believe he's so intimidated by Gwen. I wonder if he's feeling well," Val whispered back. She glanced over her shoulder to see John sitting in the first row of bleachers. He winked at her, and she smiled. Constance, catching the whole exchange, grinned at Val.

"I see you and the handsome Mr. Hatfield are still an item," Constance chuckled. "You're the talk of the town."

Val blushed a little. "It's certainly difficult to date a local celebrity without everyone knowing about it." She'd settled into her newfound fame much more easily than she would have thought.

"So what's he like?" Constance asked, her eyes bright with intrigue.

"What can I say? He's positively wonderful, and I'm pretty much crazy about him." Val smiled broadly. Refocusing her thoughts on John made her happy.

"I'm so happy for you two, Val," Constance said.

The lights dimmed, and people shuffled quickly to their seats. A hush fell over the crowd, and the evening began. Gwen and Roger sat in armchairs on the stage with the moderator seated between them. Kent welcomed the audience, briefly discussed the ground rules, and then plowed right into the first wave of questions.

By the third question, Gwen had hit her stride, creating an easy rapport with the moderator and engaging the audience. Barton relaxed a good deal and started to ease into his normal charismatic politician persona. As a result, the debate was exciting, the opponents well matched. Barton relied heavily on his experience and Gwen spoke about the optimistic possibilities.

Midway through the debate, the topic of finances came up. The first questions dealt mostly with the normal fiscal responsibilities of the mayor, and both candidates handled them with ease. Then the moderator broached the topic of accountability for official spending. The easy tone which Barton had been answering questions grew strained. He struggled to keep himself calm while barreling through answers as vaguely as possible.

Gwen focused deliberately and with care on her own belief in government transparency, avoiding any reference to the current situation. The moment was pregnant with tension. Val looked over and could see Kathy Barton breathing in gulps. As much as Val disliked Barton, his palpable discomfort made her feel another small amount of compassion for him and his wife. The look of concern on Kathy's face made clear this scandal had deeply affected her husband.

Then the moment ended, and questions moved on to social issues where the differences between the candidates became much more apparent. When it came to the nuts and bolts of city governance, Barton and Gwen didn't actually stand on opposite sides of the fence. Gwen was often noted as being a fiscal conservative, and it made her views similar to Barton's. In fact, in council matters, Barton and Gwen often found themselves supporting the same actions. On social issues, Gwen's beliefs became much more liberal. She believed in and supported social programs far beyond the scope of Barton's much more conservative views.

Barton seemed to take hold of these differences. His answers became pointedly argumentative, and his animation contained an edge of desperation. He reached out to his base in hopes of saving himself. Gwen stayed calm, even when Barton's answers bordered on personal, and, in the end, she came off as the more rational and reasonable of the two.

To conclude the debate, each candidate received a few moments to sway the voters with statements on any topic. And while Barton's plea stayed firmly grounded in his own qualities, the angry tone sounded in his voice.

The house lights came on and people filed out of the

auditorium. Val watched Barton stand shakily and walk toward Kathy, who gave him a hug, and they walked out of the building, arm in arm. Val was conflicted. It was much easier to vilify Barton when he wasn't behaving like a broken and angry man. It occurred to Val, not for the first time, that despite his bravado, Barton was an ordinary man at the end of each day.

"What an interesting debate," Constance said. The governor's wife stood beside Val, watching the crowd.

"Yes, it was. I thought Gwen did a great job." Val waved at Gwen who went back to her conversation with Kent.

"I spoke with Kathy yesterday, and she said Roger is absolutely furious with Gwen."

Turning to Constance, Val frowned and asked, "Why is he so mad at Gwen?"

"Because he thinks she leaked the travel audit to the press," Constance said, very matter-of-fact.

"She didn't," Val said, feeling angry. "Gwen actually thought the press made too much of it."

Constance smiled sadly. "I think Roger is hell-bent on seeing Gwen as the enemy. I doubt he'd care whether she really leaked it."

Val knew Constance was probably right, but it didn't make her feel less irate. "Of course he doesn't care about the actual truth," Val said, bitterly.

Constance nodded and continued, "The governor has been sympathizing with Roger." Constance referred to her husband by his title whenever she thought him a jerk. Clearly they had exchanged words on the topic. "Of course, it's hard to be sympathetic when Roger's behavior is so out-of-control."

Val sighed, "There's probably no talking to him about it. I suppose we'll have to let the whole thing work itself out."

"Do you mind if I stop by your office Monday afternoon?" Constance asked. "I'm going to be downtown, and I thought maybe we could meet up."

"Sure, what time? I should be back from campaign headquarters by five on Monday," Val said.

"Sometime after 5:30? I'll come by when I'm done. Maybe we can have dinner?" Constance asked. Val nodded as John walked up to stand beside her. Constance's smile grew wider, and she said "Hello, Mr. Hatfield."

"Mrs. Carlton," John replied sweetly. "Please call me John. Looks like we'll be running into each other a lot." He seemed amused by her formality and could practically see the wheels in her head spin.

The governor, having finished a conversation near the stage, walked over to Constance and put his arm around her waist. "Come on, sweetheart. Let's go grab a drink." Spying John, he added, "Hi, John. How are you? And you, Val?" Without waiting for an answer, he turned back to Constance, "I'm exhausted. Let's go."

Constance rolled her eyes and took his hand, following him toward the exit.

John chuckled. "I bet he's an interesting man to be married to."

Val smiled, kissing him on the cheek. "I don't think I'd want to try it."

"Yes, I'd rather you didn't," he smirked. "I have other plans for you."

Val's heart fluttered, and she slid her fingers between John's, giving his hand a squeeze.

Gwen finally headed off the stage. When she reached them, she exclaimed, "Am I glad that's over! Sheesh. Let's go get a drink, or chocolate, or something."

They all headed to the parking lot. Gwen stopped every few moments to say "hello" to someone congratulating her on the performance or wishing her well.

When they finally reached her car, Gwen looked at John and asked, "Can I borrow Val for a few minutes?" She smiled sweetly.

"Sure, I'll meet you ladies at Andy's, if that sounds good?"

They nodded, and Val climbed into Gwen's car, glancing back to wave at John.

"You did great tonight, Gwen," Val said as they drove.

"Thanks. I had a great time. Except …" She paused, apparently looking for the right words. Val waited patiently. "Okay. Look, Val, I want you to promise to stay calm." Val's shoulders tensed. "Right before the debate started, Barton took me aside and threatened me." Her voice trailed off at the end of the statement, as if by turning down the volume she could soften the blow for Val. It didn't work.

"Excuse me?" Val's voice rose. "What in the world? What did he say?"

"Well, I believe his exact words were, 'I know what you did, and I promise you, you're going to regret it. You need to leave the politics to the men.' I told him I had no idea what he was talking about and he needed to back off. Can you believe that?"

"Constance says he thinks you leaked the travel audit to the press," Val said.

Gwen said, seething, "What a jerk! Of course I didn't!"

"I know. I'm sure Roger doesn't give a damn. He's looking for reasons to hate you. Constance said she talked to Kathy yesterday."

"Well, I suppose that solves the mystery. I was starting to think he'd gone crazy," Gwen said.

They pulled into the parking lot at Andy's to find John had beaten them there. They walked in, found a corner table, and proceeded to wolf down a huge piece of chocolate molten lava cake, split three ways, and some wine all around. With bellies full of chocolate, exhaustion set in. They paid the bill, and John took Val home.

They spent the weekend holed up in her apartment, watching television, cuddling, spending time in bed, and avoiding the world together. By Sunday evening, it was almost easy to imagine they were the only two people in the world.

Curled up under a blanket on the couch, John turned to Val and said, "So, I was thinking maybe we could take my mother out for dinner this weekend. I want you to meet her."

"I already met her, remember?" Val teased.

"Um, yes, well. What I mean is ..." he said nervously. "I'd like to introduce you to my mother as my *girlfriend.*" He looked and sounded like a teenager, and Val found his sudden case of nerves irresistible.

"When?" she asked, sweetly.

He smiled. "Saturday night? I thought maybe we could go to The Lodge."

The Lodge was undoubtedly the most exclusive and near-ly-impossible-to-get-reservations-at restaurant in Cambria. *Well, maybe not if you're John Hatfield,* Val thought to herself, smiling. She'd gone there exactly once, for her sister's wedding rehearsal dinner. The thought of this as a casual date was ludicrous. She was suddenly nervous there was more to this dinner invitation than she'd expected.

She swallowed. "Um, sure. Yes." Then she nuzzled her face into John's chest, trying not to let him see the color creeping into her cheeks. He stroked her hair tenderly, and they settled in for the rest of the evening. Around nine, John stirred. He needed to head home because he was out of clean clothes, and he had to go to work early the next morning. Val groaned as John eased himself off the couch.

"You want to come with me?" His eyes twinkled as he asked.

Temptation. Val wanted nothing more than to go with him, but she had an early day as well and needed to do some laundry. Reluctantly, they said their goodbyes.

CHAPTER 14

Breakfast burrito and coffee in hand, Val arrived at her office early Monday morning. Gwen would stop by around ten for their daily strategy session. In the meantime, Val had about a week's worth of other work to fit in. She raced against the clock, and when Gwen walked through the door she felt pretty good about her progress.

They headed out for an early lunch and then over to campaign headquarters to check on canvassing efforts. Victoria was sending volunteers out the door when they arrived and greeted Gwen with a smile and the latest poll numbers.

"This is it, Gwen." Victoria handed her a report before Gwen even made it to her desk. "We're ahead by six points!"

Val and Gwen both gasped. Only a few weeks ago, it would have taken a miracle to catch up. Thank goodness for miracles!

"I almost feel bad for Roger," Gwen said, putting her purse down and leaning back in her chair. "He had this election in the bag. As much as I believe I'm the better candidate, we would have struggled to win."

"Well, it's not like it's been easy," Val said. As exciting as the campaign had been, exhaustion had set in, and they knew there wouldn't be many breaks now until election day.

"I know," Gwen said, "But without Roger's recent extreme outbursts and horrible behavior, we'd have had to fight to gain any ground. And did you see him at the debate? He looked awful!"

Victoria nodded in agreement. "He actually looked ill. And his wife looked just as bad. She watched him like a hawk through the whole thing."

"I wonder what's going on with him?" Val murmured. She thought about her father and the severity of his depression. In a way, understanding his situation only increased her concern over Barton's crazy behavior.

"Well, I thought you were absolutely amazing at the debate," Victoria said to Gwen, her voice dripping with admiration. Victoria had worked on Gwen's campaign for city council as well, so she was as big a Gwen supporter as they came.

"It was so much fun," Gwen said – she'd always loved a good debate, "and nice to actually answer some questions that didn't attack me on the basis of my age."

Val nodded. "You did wonderfully! Now, enough ego-stroking. Let's get to work. We haven't won this election yet."

At two that afternoon, the first of the voter information sessions started with a remarkable turnout. The tiny office overflowed with a continual stream of constituents. Val took copious notes as questions came up, making special notations of topics that could be covered in more general terms on social media or in press releases. It proved both exhausting and exhilarating. Two hours later, the last of the stragglers finally left, and Val decided to return to her office to get some more work done before Constance arrived.

* * *

Val was working busily when there was a knock at her office door. She looked at her clock – only a little after five.

"Come in!" she said thinking Constance's meeting had let out early. Instead, she was taken aback to see Roger Barton walk into her office, leaving the door slightly ajar.

"Hello, Ms. Shakely," he said. Not waiting to be invited, he took a seat in the chair nearest Val's desk. His action violated her personal space, but she kept her expression stern.

"What can I do for you, Mayor?" Val said, formally. His appearance, unannounced, unnerved her. The last time he'd visited her office was almost five years ago when she'd declined to take him on as a client. He was livid then, and his last words to her had been anything but kind.

"Well, first you can explain to me why a woman who doesn't take on political clients seems to have made herself quite comfortable in the enemy camp." His words dripped with anger, and though she could feel her blood pressure on the rise, Val determined to keep her words calm and professional. The campaign neared its end. Why hadn't he confronted her about this sooner?

"Who I accept as a client isn't any of your business, Mayor," she said, coolly.

He smiled viciously. "I hear not all of your clients are happy with your choice." He tried to pick a fight, but she refused to take the bait.

"I couldn't say – I don't usually talk to my clients about politics," she said simply.

Barton's face flushed further. He made a special effort to put Val off her game, and her failure to respond made him angry. She realized his entire visit was meant to intimidate her, and she wouldn't let him succeed in his mission.

"You know, your cousin is a lying sack of shit," he hissed. "She pretends to be all honesty and integrity, but she plays the game just like the rest of us."

"Mr. Barton, whatever you think Gwen has done, she didn't. And I would appreciate it if you wouldn't use that type of language in *my* office," she replied curtly. Val wasn't known for being confrontational. She could feel her face burning, though she wasn't willing to give an inch, especially here in her own office, her safe place.

Barton stood and paced. He looked at Val's posters and perused her bookshelves in silence, tension mounting. It was like watching a caged animal, and as the moments passed, Val's apprehension grew.

"If there's nothing I can do for you, I'd appreciate if you would leave. I have a lot of work to do," Val said, standing and getting ready to move to the door to escort her unwanted visitor out of her office.

Quickly and unexpectedly, Barton stepped between Val and the door. She stepped back to make some space between them. Barton moved as well, forcing Val to retreat toward the office's window. She found herself trapped behind her desk. Barton stood about a head taller than Val, and he loomed above her, menacing.

She shrank. Suddenly, she was afraid. Barton's demeanor in the past week had been increasingly angry and agitated. She'd never felt fear like she did now, pinned between her desk and this hulking man who terrified her.

"Mr. Barton," she said slowly through gritted teeth, "you need to leave my office. Right now." Her voice shook. She stared at him coldly, praying for the strength to make it through this ordeal.

He didn't flinch. Instead, he inched closer. In a slow and malicious tone, he said, "you and your pretty cousin think you can make a fool out of me. Well, I promise you, it's not going to happen." He leaned so close she could feel his breath hot on her cheek. Her hands shook, and her mind raced. She wasn't a fighter but she started to wonder whether she could kick and scream her way out of his situation.

"Roger," Val softened her tone, trying a different tack. The look on Barton's face was murderous. "Roger. Please. You need to leave now." Nothing. No response. He was stuck on the verge of something dangerous and, despite her fear, Val found herself pondering what could be going on in his mind.

Then, from behind Barton came a woman's voice. "Roger?"

Val's whole body practically screamed with relief as Constance walked into the office. The tension in Barton's body seemed to recede, and he leaned away from Val, the spell broken.

Constance moved toward Barton, taking his arm and firmly pulling him away from Val. Her eyes were cold and ice dripped from her words as she growled, "I believe Ms. Shakely asked you to leave." Her tone left no room for argument.

Barton looked stunned, confused. It took him a moment to recognize Constance, and once he did, all the color rushed out of his face. He nearly ran as he dashed out the door.

Val sank into her chair. Tears slid in huge wet drips down her face. Her body shook, her heart raced. Constance pulled a chair beside Val and wrapped her arms around her friend, rubbing her back and making soothing sounds. It took nearly ten minutes for Val to stop sobbing.

"Oh, God. If you hadn't come in ..." She stopped short, the reality of the danger she'd experienced too terrifying for her mind to wrap itself around.

"It's going to be all right," Constance said, soothingly. Val felt like a scared child, and she found Constance's arms strangely comforting. Val realized she hadn't been comforted by her own mother for a long time, and her heart ached. Constance whispered, "Call John. I think we'd better take a rain check on dinner tonight."

Val nodded and picked up her phone. When John answered, she choked back tears and handed the phone to Constance who said, "John? It's Constance Carlton. I need you to come to Val's office and take her home."

John's office was twenty minutes away. He must have raced out the moment he hung up the phone, because he was there in no time at all. When John saw Val slumped in her chair, his expression turned from concern to alarm. Constance told him what she'd seen, what she'd walked into. John thanked her for calling him and took her place, wrapping his arms around Val, and she melted into another fit of sobs, thankful to have him there. Constance said goodbye and headed out, grim-faced.

John had never experienced anger like he did at that moment, and he was unprepared. He didn't know what to say, so he held Val and breathed and waited. She finally lifted her head, reached for a tissue, and took a deep breath, willing herself to calm down. "Will you walk me home?" she said, her voice shaking.

"I wouldn't let you out of my sight under any circumstances," John said, his jaw set firmly. He looked like his face might break apart from tension, but luckily Val didn't notice. He kissed her cheek and helped her into her coat.

They walked quickly in the chilly fall evening – Val weak and in shock. When they reached her apartment, John bundled her up on the couch and asked her what had happened.

"While I worked, I waited for Constance to stop by for dinner. Someone knocked. I thought it was her. Roger walked in, and it made me angry. He tried to intimidate me, but when I asked him to leave, he backed me into the corner. He said Gwen and I made him look foolish, and we'd regret it."

She took a long slow breath and continued. "I really seemed like he'd kill me. The look in his eyes ..." she shuddered. "It sounds silly when I say it, but I think he wanted to hurt me." She started to feel numb. John got up and made her a cup of tea.

After a few minutes of silence, John said, "I think you should call the police."

Val shook her head. "He didn't actually do anything to me. I don't know what I'd tell them." She sounded defeated thinking about her options.

"You'll tell them Barton attacked you. Constance can back you up." John's voice was tense, his face etched with barely concealed fury.

"I don't want to go through that," Val said, sighing. "I just want him to stay away from me."

John thought for a minute. "I'll talk to him."

Val looked at him, concerned. "I don't think that's a good idea, John. You look like you could kill him."

John had to admit he couldn't think straight.

"Anyway, I don't want to do anything tonight. I want to sleep. Will you stay with me?" she asked

"You'd have to pry me loose to get me to leave," he said, allowing himself to relax a little bit.

* * *

Val woke up in a furious mood. John tried to soothe her, but she couldn't be comforted. She'd never experienced something like it before. She shook with rage. The old Val, the one who'd been content to sit on the sidelines of life, would have crumpled under the pressure of this trauma, but the new empowered Val was extremely irate. *This* Val understood Barton had tried to take away her power, and she wouldn't give it up. After a life-time of cowering, Val was finally ready to stand up for herself.

She showered, dressed, and joined John in the kitchen. "On second thought, I think I'd like to talk to the police."

John nodded, relieved. He took a shower, put on the previous evening's clothes, and they went to the police station. While they waited to talk to someone, Val's phone started buzzing. It was Gwen. Val sent her a quick text telling her she couldn't talk and would see her at campaign headquarters at noon.

She held John's hand, thankful for his support. Val could tell he was stressed, and she couldn't blame him. She still didn't quite know what to make of the whole incident herself. She'd never thought of Barton as a violent man. Mean spirited, yes. A hothead, absolutely. His outburst against Val made her wonder what he was capable of. Val didn't know if the police could do anything, but she knew if she didn't put it on record, it would haunt her. And she tired of being haunted.

A young officer came out to escort them to a conference room. Val told her story and wasn't surprised when the officer informed her of what a long shot pressing charges would be. Even though Constance had walked in, the fact remained Barton hadn't touched Val. She could press charges for harassment. It would come down to his word against hers, and honestly, Val didn't want to get involved in a legal battle with one of the most powerful men in town.

The officer assured Val they would talk to Barton. He also informed her she could file a restraining order against him if she felt threatened. Val declined. The look on Barton's face when Constance entered the scene convinced her that he knew he'd gone too far.

After leaving the station, John took Val out for coffee. She finally was hungry, and she gobbled down a bagel thickly coated with cream cheese. They made small talk, the air between them heavy with tension.

Finally, John said, "I'm sorry, Val, I need to tell you something."

Val tensed. She didn't know what he'd say, but she felt too raw for bad news. "Sure."

"Last night scared the hell out of me. I know it's probably crazy, but something horrible could have happened, and I should have been there." He poured his heart out, laying his emotions on the table. "Honestly, I'm afraid to leave your side today." His face was tight with tension.

Much to his surprise, Val smiled. Even more shocking, she laughed. John gave her a quizzical look. Unexpectedly, he laughed, too. Before long they were roaring, causing quite a scene in the coffee shop. The tension finally broke, and the stress bubbled out in a rush of guffaws. Val laughed so hard her head ached.

Eventually, they settled down, taking deep breaths in an attempt to regain some composure. "Well, that wasn't quite the reaction I had expected," John chuckled, his face sore from smiling. "I love you," he said, rubbing her arm.

She beamed at him, "I love you, too."

CHAPTER 15

Laughter may just be the best medicine, Val thought when she entered campaign headquarters. John had insisted on dropping her off, which she found both annoying and endearing, and she wondered if he actually intended to escort her through every minute of the day.

While amusing, Val felt bad for John. In a way, he feared the situation more than she did, which, when she thought about it, seemed strange. The appearance of John in her life made her more secure. And his fear of losing her convinced Val of the depth of his feelings. In an absurd way, Barton's attack had strengthened their bond. As happy as Val was with John, she suspected her unexpected resilience had a lot to do with her growing sense of strength and confidence.

Val was met by two stony faces in Gwen's office. Her cousin's, ashen and furious, and Constance's, which held only slightly more color. Val sighed. She'd known she would have to tell Gwen about the attack sooner or later, but she wasn't quite prepared to have the discussion yet. She knew the whole situation would derail the day's activities.

"Val, are you okay? Why didn't you call me?" Gwen's voice betrayed a hint of hurt.

"I was in shock most of the night. John stayed over, and I pretty much did nothing but sleep."

She recounted the story once again, starting from the moment

Barton walked into her office and ending with her morning visit to the police. Gwen looked relieved to hear the police had gotten involved, but she couldn't hide the worry lines cutting through her forehead like a knife.

Voice shaking, Gwen said, "I'm appalled. Stunned. I have no love for Roger, but I never would have imagined him getting physical." Gwen shook her head as if the movement could somehow make it all a bad dream or misunderstanding.

"I know what you mean." Val leaned her head back in the chair for a minute and took a long deep breath. Talking about the incident took away some of the pain and fear, but it still remained a little surreal – an awful dream. Constance, who'd been sitting quietly, finally spoke up.

"Val, I paid Roger a visit this morning." Constance proceeded with caution as she watched Val's eyebrows rise a little. She continued, "He looked grave, and though he didn't apologize for his actions, it seemed clear he looked for some sort of absolution. I told him if he so much as looked at you or Gwen with anything less than complete professionalism and respect I would be talking with the police."

Val's eyes were wide, though she couldn't suppress a grin. "Good grief. What did he say?"

"Nothing. Literally. He nodded, and I left without giving him a chance to say another word." Constance had a satisfied look on her face. "What could he say, Val? He behaved like a monster last night. Roger's lucky I walked in and not John. The look on John's face when he got to your office was so intense." She chuckled. "I believe Mr. Hatfield is pretty crazy about you."

Val tried to imagine the expression on Barton's face when Constance walked into his office. Having been caught was bad enough, but being reprimanded, and by a woman no less, had to have been demoralizing. Val was actually relieved it had been Constance and not John who talked with Barton. She had to admit she could understand John's emotions. Barton's verbal jabs at Gwen had been enough to make Val see red, and she couldn't even imagine how she would have reacted had he attacked Gwen.

Gwen still looked shaken. "Nonetheless," she started, "I don't think we should let this go."

"What can we do, Gwen?" Val said, trying to soothe her. "I filed a report with the police, and, quite frankly, he didn't touch me, so I'm not sure there's much they could do to him anyway. I'm good." And even Val was a little surprised to find this was true. She was proud of herself for having confronted this horrible situation without letting it suffocate her.

Unmoved, Gwen said, "Well, you're not working in your office alone anymore." She crossed her arms in a childish huff.

Val forced a laugh. "Don't you start that, too! John's already insisted on escorting me everywhere. I'm surprised he even let me come to work today." Val tried to lighten the mood, but she could see Gwen didn't want to let it go.

"Come on, Val, this is serious. He attacked you! It's frightening!" Gwen's voice rose, and Val realized how much this had shaken her cousin.

Val walked over to Gwen, wrapped her arms around her neck, and showered her cheek with tiny kisses until Gwen finally started to giggle. "I know you're upset, Gwen, and I am, too, but here's what we're going to do. We're going to work on this campaign, and you're going to stomp all over Roger Barton in this election. He'll learn he can't treat people like this when you win by a landslide." Val looked her cousin right in the eye and winked.

"Well, let's get started then, I guess," Gwen said rather reluctantly.

* * *

With the election one week away, Gwen's campaign office was in a constant state of motion. Gwen's volunteers were dedicated, and with so many of them, they made short work of an incredible amount of canvassing. Well-attended voter information sessions, the campaign website, and social media sites saw increased followers. By Friday afternoon, Gwen led Barton by almost ten points, an unimaginably huge margin.

Val had finally convinced John she would be alright walking to and from her office, though he insisted on staying with her every night. Secretly, she loved having him around so much, but she still made a daily effort to get him back into a normal routine for his sanity's sake.

Intellectually, Val had put the incident behind her. Of course, that didn't stop her from locking the office door. She'd made an appointment to talk to a therapist before Barton had attacked, and now she was glad she did. Her sense of security had been rocked. Even though he hadn't laid a hand on her, Barton's physical presence invading her personal space generated a feeling she couldn't quite shake.

Her first visit with Tracy, the counselor, was Friday afternoon. Val liked her immediately. Tracy's calm and straightforward approach put Val at ease, allowing her to open up more naturally. She left the therapist's office with new coping tools and a sense of peace she'd never felt before.

John and Val spent Friday evening with Gwen at the campaign office. Gwen held a "whether we win or lose" celebration to thank her staff and volunteers for their hard work. The mood was festive, and around ten, when the crowd started to disperse, Val felt reinvigorated. She, Gwen, and John decided to catch a late movie and relax. It was a wonderful, fun, and exhilarating time.

Val spent the night with John at his apartment. The next morning, they awoke to sunlight streaming in through his bedroom windows and lounged. Later, Val met her cousin to shop for a new dress. Since meeting John, her wardrobe had expanded greatly, and though she hated to admit it, she began to like all the fancy shopping trips. Meeting John's mother weighed heavily on her mind. Even though things with her own mother had begun to improve, she was never particularly comfortable in formal family gatherings. Val knew John and his mother were close, and she desperately wanted the woman to like her.

The duo headed uptown to shop in boutiques they never would have imagined setting foot in before. Val wanted to look nothing short of stunning tonight. She had always lived simply, keeping her expenses low, perhaps due to her general business anxiety. She had worked hard to reach a comfortable level of financial stability. She could afford the splurge, and this occasion called for some primping. In the time they'd been dating, John had seen her in everything from the legendary blue dress to sweats. This week, he'd seen her at her worst, and she wanted him to see her at her best as well.

Val tried on literally dozens of dresses and pairs of shoes before deciding on an emerald cocktail dress far less conservative than any garment she'd ever owned. Its scoop back revealed an amount of skin she never felt comfortable showing in the past. She loved the way John's hands moved on her back. She hoped the dress encouraged numerous touches.

Val's expression alternated between smiles and cringes as she spun in front of the mirror. "I don't know, Gwen. It's awfully revealing."

Gwen chuckled. "Well, yes, but that's sort of the point, right? You're beautiful, and John's going to have a heart attack when he sees you in this!"

"But his mother's going to be there!" Val protested, not quite ready to commit.

"It's a dinner date, and you'll wear this stunning dress. I refuse to let you go home until you've paid for it and agreed to wear it!" Gwen cried, giving her cousin a good-natured nudge. "If you're going to be a society girl, you're going to have to work on dressing the part."

Val groaned. One of the drawbacks of dating a local celebrity was playing a social role not always comfortable for her. On the other hand, she looked damn good in the dress.

"Alright. You win. You always win," Val said, smiling at Gwen.

"Yes, I do," Gwen said, winking.

They went back to Val's apartment where they spent almost two hours on hair, makeup, and accessories. Val had to admit she was picture perfect tonight. She spun slowly in front of the mirror, taking in every angle and feeling wonderful. Her nerves started to get the best of her, and about ten minutes before John arrived, Gwen made her down a small glass of wine. Gwen's amusement at Val's nervousness was annoying enough to bring her back to her senses. Thank goodness for pesky cousins!

John arrived around five. Val was utterly satisfied with his jaw-dropping and sudden intake of breath when he saw her.

"You are *the* most beautiful woman," he said, moving in close and letting his hands explore her neckline and the cut of the dress on her back.

Gwen cleared her throat and John jumped. He had gotten so caught up in Val he hadn't noticed her standing two feet away. He blushed and laughed out loud. "Hi, Gwen."

"Hi, John," Gwen chuckled. "Folks, I'm outta here." As she walked past Val to the door, she stage-whispered, "And I expect a full report."

The second the door closed, John swept Val into his arms. He kissed her passionately, pulling her body close to him and feeling all her curves through her dress. Val let herself be completely absorbed in the adoration. After a few moments, she pulled away and said, her voice breathy, "We should go. We don't want to be late." She tried to compose herself. She'd never wanted to be both in a dress and out of it so badly at the same time.

John reluctantly helped Val into her coat and escorted her to his car, his arm wrapped tightly around her waist.

The Lodge, located up one of Cambria's most beautiful canyon roads, featured views overlooking the city. The winding mountain road was simply breathtaking at sunset, and Val rested her hand on John's leg as he drove, needing physical connection to keep her calm. The restaurant resided in an enormous rustic building nestled among the evergreens. The lobby décor included marble floors, leather armchairs and sofas, crystal chandeliers, and huge vases of fresh flowers everywhere despite the chilly weather. John's mother waited for them near the dining room entrance.

Anne Hatfield was the picture of elegance, known for her charitable work and her quick wit. Where John's father had been a business legend and part of Cambria's professional aristocracy, Anne occupied a place in the heart of the community. She'd been involved in practically every big charity project in Cambria for three decades, and she'd taken many politicians to task over unfulfilled promises and lack of regard for the citizens of the city. Though their paths had crossed only every now and again, Val had followed Anne's work for years, and it was both wonderful and unnerving to be standing in front of her now.

Anne watched them approach, her face warm with delight. Val relaxed.

"Hello, Mom," John said, kissing her on the cheek. "I'd like you to meet Val Shakely."

"We've met, remember?" his mother said, teasing him as Val had done. She turned and smiled warmly at Val. "It's a pleasure to see you, again." She leaned close to Val and kissed her cheek.

John beamed as he watched the two women in his life interact. They followed the host to their table, located in the middle of a huge wall of bay windows which provided a stunning view of the city. The half full dining room stirred as they made their way to their seats. Val placed her coat into the host's outstretched arms and took a seat next to John and across from Anne. She looked out the window, taking in the view.

"I've always loved this view," said Anne, gazing out the window. "When John suggested The Lodge, I was overjoyed. We come here far too infrequently."

"It's been years since I've been here," Val said, thinking of her father and her family once again. "Before my father passed away. My sister's wedding rehearsal dinner took place in the banquet hall."

"Does your sister live here?" Anne inquired.

"No. Charleston, South Carolina, with her husband and children. My mother lives there as well."

"Do you have any family in Cambria?" Anne continued.

"Just Gwen. She's my cousin." Val didn't know how much John had told his mother, so she assumed an interrogation may occur.

"Oh, yes, our future mayor." Anne grinned. "I recall John mentioning your relationship some weeks ago. Seems the campaign is going well."

"Yes, it's both exciting and nerve wracking, but I think Gwen has an excellent chance of winning."

John added, "She's ahead ten points in the polls. Her chances appear more than excellent." He smiled at Val.

Anne studied the look between Val and John. "So, John, what's kept you busy these past few weeks? I've hardly seen you." The knowing grin on her face betrayed her. John blushed and cleared his throat.

"Well, I've spent a lot of time with someone very special to me." He looked at Val, a serious expression coming over his face. "And I hope to continue spending my time with her."

Val's cheeks commenced their normal burn. John reached over and took her hand, lacing his fingers with hers.

Hoping to put Val at ease, Anne smiled.

"You know, Val, I think The Lodge has the best Waldorf salad I've ever tasted."

Val relaxed, and they began discussing food choices and wine. They feasted on salads and stuffed mushrooms, perfectly prepared steaks and seafood, and finished the night with some of the most delectable desserts Val had ever seen. John's mother was charming and approachable. She asked Val all about her family and work and then offered some wonderful and funny stories about John as a child.

Val was enjoying herself so much, she was completely unprepared for John's sudden shift in mood. He became visibly agitated, and his mother finally interrupted. "John, dear, what in the world is bothering you?"

John smiled, timidly, realizing his brooding had translated to his face. "Val?"

She gulped, completely thrown off-guard by the shift in his demeanor. His face all seriousness and nerves. "John?" It was all she could think to say.

And then he launched in, words exploding in a torrent of nervous energy. "I know you're probably going to think I'm crazy when I say this, but these last few months – and this week in particular – has convinced me that I want to spend the rest of my life making you smile, making you happy, keeping you safe." He swallowed hard. He sounded horribly sappy and didn't know how to make it less clichéd. Maybe it didn't matter. "I'm in love with you. I want to marry you. Will you marry me, Val?"

Val's expression showed shock and wonderment. Anne, on the other hand, looked positively unsurprised. As a child, when John made a decision, he embraced it with confidence and gusto.

Val, on the other hand, had trouble finding words to speak. She also wanted to spend her life with John. But it was crazy! They'd only known each other a few months, and their relationship had been riddled with drama. What did Val know about marriage anyway? Considering how little she'd dated, she hadn't given much thought in a long time to what she would say or how she would feel if proposed to. She didn't know how to react.

All these thoughts stormed through Val's mind in a matter of seconds while she sat, jaw clenched tightly, willing herself to be calm and collected but failing to prevent tears forming in her eyes. John looked concerned, barely breathing, and she realized he waited for her to speak.

Looking deep into his eyes, Val studied John. She saw the strong and confident man she loved and also the boy his mother had been talking about, wanting his father's approval and never quite measuring up. Her heart neared the bursting point. She *was* in love with John, and she *wanted* to spend the rest of her life with him. Her over-analytical brain tried its best to create a list of pro's and con's, but her heart won the battle.

She smiled broadly, seeing John's face relax as she did, and said, "Yes, I believe I will."

CHAPTER 16

"Gwen?" Val looked at her phone to see if the call had been dropped, but the connection remained. "Can you hear me?" Silence.

She started to hang up and try again when she heard a high-pitched squeal on the other end of the line. Val's concerned expression turned to a grin when she realized she'd rendered her chatterbox cousin speechless. Finally, Gwen squeezed out enough breath to gasp, "Are you kidding me?"

Val laughed out loud. "Would I joke about something so incredible?" Val looked down at her left hand and studied the sparkling ring John had placed on her finger Saturday night. She had spent more time than she cared to admit staring at the ring. The memory of his proposal, fresh in her mind, sent shivers through her body. By Sunday afternoon, when they finally rolled out of bed, John jabbed gently at Val every time he caught her staring, transfixed by the twinkling diamond on her hand.

After she'd said yes, John's mother had come around the table to give her new daughter-in-law-to-be a huge hug. Val felt herself instantly becoming a part of something quite special. John's enormous smile seemed almost comical. The rest of the evening was joyful, and when John and Val returned to his apartment, they spent the entire night and most of the next morning basking in their happiness, making love, sleeping completely entangled, waking up to kisses and caresses, and then doing it all over again. Val's bliss enveloped her whole being and wrapped itself like a protective pillow around her heart, leaving her with a bright outlook on the future.

A throat clearing from the other end of the line interrupted her reverie. Val realized she'd gone silent, lost in her daydreams, leaving Gwen waiting impatiently.

"Sorry, Gwen," Val chuckled. "I guess I'm still in a state of shock."

"Can I come over? Are you home?" Gwen asked.

"Yes, and yes. John dropped me off this afternoon. I ran out of clean clothes." Val had returned to her apartment to do laundry and get ready for the week, but she mostly sat on her couch staring at her ring. "I need to do laundry. Want to watch a movie?"

"Yep. I'll pick up a pizza." Gwen hung up before Val could say another word. She gathered her dirty clothes and started a load of laundry, thankful for her apartment's stackable washer and dryer, which afforded her the luxury of staying in her pajamas while washing her clothes.

Gwen showed up thirty minutes later holding a pizza and a bottle of wine. She ditched the food and drink as quickly as she could on Val's kitchen table, wheeled around, grabbed Val's hand, and admired her ring. Val feigned annoyance, snatching her hand back and giggling.

Gwen bubbled, "Oh, Val, you realize you're going to be Mrs. John Hatfield. Married to the elusive, reclusive, never-before-tamed heartthrob ... you're never going to have a moment's peace again! Every woman in town will hate you!"

Gwen's excitement was contagious, and despite her already elated state of being, Val's heart started to race again.

"I'm still so amazed." Val plopped down on the couch. "Last night was a dream. I still keep thinking I made the whole thing up, but then I look at the ring. His mother's as wonderful as I ever imagined her to be." Val took some calming breaths, eyes still locked on her finger.

Gwen sat down beside Val. "So, what did he say?"

"He said he's in love with me, wanted to marry me, and he knows the whole thing sounded crazy!" Val chuckled. "He looked like he'd have a heart attack before he asked. That man may actually be more high-strung than me." Val smiled affectionately, picturing John's sweet smile and trying not to get too caught up in the memories of the passionate night that followed.

"I'm so happy for you, Val! Have you told your mom?" Gwen asked.

"Um, no, actually. I didn't even tell her I'd been dating anyone." Val looked sheepishly at her cousin. "What do you think she'll say?"

"She'll be thrilled, trust me." Gwen said, reassuringly. Val got the feeling her cousin had been filling Val's mother in on the details of her life.

Val picked up her phone and dialed her mother's number; another unscheduled call with another hesitant but happy greeting. In the weeks since her near breakdown, Val and her mother had spoken more regularly. Their conversations still tended to stay on safe, shallow topics, but they made progress. Val told her mom the whole story, and her mother got very quiet.

"Mom? You okay?"

Val could hear some sniffling and realized her mom was crying. "Oh, honey, I'm so happy for you."

Val was overcome with emotion. She'd spent so many years distancing herself from her family, and now she realized how much she needed and wanted her mother to be a part of her life. "Do you have Thanksgiving plans?"

Before she knew it, Val's family was coming for Thanksgiving. Apparently, her mother had already been talking to her sister about planning a visit, and on hearing Val's news, her mother resolved it would happen sooner rather than later. A few more calls and plans developed to have a big family Thanksgiving at Anne's house. John's siblings, neither of whom Val had met, and Val's mom and sister would all be there. Val waited for the inevitable sense of dread, and was surprised when it didn't come. Life was good.

In honor of the upcoming nuptials, Gwen and Val tossed in their favorite wedding-themed chick flick, munched on pizza, and chattered busily about the holidays. John joined them around eight. He'd lasted only a few hours before deciding he didn't want to be away from his beloved for a whole night. He appeared on Val's doorstep, overnight bag in hand, and Gwen made her escape with Val's promise to meet her bright and early the next morning.

* * *

Election eve was sunny and warm for the season. Val and Gwen met for coffee early and headed to campaign headquarters. Volunteers arrived earlier than usual, and the whole room soon buzzed. Many of the volunteers who'd canvassed the week before planned to stand on street corners and in front of retail businesses holding signs, urging voters to head to the polls the next day. Some prepared for a full day as poll workers. The city had set up a small number of centralized polling places as mail-in voting had resulted in relatively low turnout for in-person voting on election day.

Gwen planned a catered election night party at the Hyatt Regency ballroom to watch the election results and celebrate. The polls showed Gwen maintaining an average ten-point lead over Barton. Barring some major unforeseen disaster, the general opinion declared Gwen would take the election by a healthy margin. Gwen erred on the side of caution. Despite her dislike for Barton, she knew she'd need the support of his conservative base in her new role

Since his disastrous visit to Val's office the week before, Barton's presence in the media had been substantially minimalized, causing Val to wonder whether his campaign team had started to prepare for his eventual defeat. They pulled the entire ad campaign attacking Gwen's inexperience. His nightly sound bites, previously filled with venom and condescension, turned meek and humble. The changing tone in Barton's campaign seemed to stop Gwen's polling success in its tracks.

The Barton campaign had reverted to a message of merit and dropped the personal attacks and smear campaign at the eleventh hour. Val found herself wondering whether Barton had a change of heart, or whether he was running scared. Either way, it looked as if politics as usual would lose the election this time around.

At a late lunch, Val, Gwen, and several campaign staff members discussed the next twenty-four hours. Gwen needed to be visible on election day, so Val had scheduled her to visit the library, attend a women's business luncheon, interview with the newspaper, and spend the rest of the afternoon and evening at the Hyatt, meeting with constituents and answering last minute emails. It would be a harrowing day with many moving parts.

The group went back to the office to finalize schedules and ensure every team leader had all the pertinent information. Having made backup contact lists to cover their bases, Gwen and Val locked up around seven and headed home.

Gwen's energy was nearly manic, and though she had wanted to hang out for a while, Val made her drive home and promise to go to sleep. She texted Gwen about half an hour later and gave her one last motherly reminder to get to bed. Gwen assured her she'd go to sleep after a mug of hot tea, though Val was less than convinced.

After straightening up a bit, Val got into her coziest pajamas and nestled into bed with a book. The first night in many she hadn't slept next to John, and she missed him. She kept trying to tell herself she would get to wake up to him every morning before she knew it and should relish these last days of being alone. She wanted to be near him always.

John had flown to Seattle early that morning for an unexpected emergency management meeting. Two times in two weeks and he wasn't terribly thrilled about it. John loved his business but had recent troubles with the Northwest branch manager. The man had finally quit with no notice about a month ago, and John's presence was required more frequently while they hired and trained a replacement.

He'd fly back home Tuesday, before the polls closed, and planned on heading straight from the airport to the Hyatt. Val knew she'd be busy every minute, but she still couldn't help but pout a little at having to wait so long to see him.

She finished the last few pages of her book and lay down to sleep. As she started to doze, her phone buzzed. Grumpily, she sat up, switched on her light, and reached for the phone. It was Gwen.

I can't sleep!!! Help!!!

Val chuckled. *Want to have a sleepover?*

I'm way ahead of you.

On cue, the doorbell rang. Val hopped out of bed and let her soon-to-be-mayor, pajama clad cousin into the apartment.

"You know, this won't be easy to do when you're an old married woman," Gwen noted as she set up a temporary sleeping station on the couch.

"Tell you what," Val said, squeezing Gwen's hand. "We'll work on getting you hitched as soon as we get you elected."

Val chuckled, said goodnight, and went back to bed.

* * *

The sleepover did both women a world of good. Val woke ready to face the day despite having missed John. And Gwen actually got some sleep, a miracle given her level of anxiety. Gwen had a cheerful and enthusiastic disposition, and it was a rare thing to see her flustered. This campaign had provided a lot more opportunities to see her cousin off-guard than Val had predicted, and she was glad she'd soon be back to normal, perky Gwen. Her cousin was her rock, and despite the positive turns Val's life had taken, she wanted her rock back in place.

They decided to grab breakfast burritos on the way to the Century Building. Val's usual breakfast stop hadn't seen much of her lately, and the owner practically shouted with glee at seeing them walk through the door. Val blushed a little, realizing how rigid she'd been in some of her pre-John routines. She began to feel flexible, adaptable. Funny to think her breakfast choices could provide an opportunity for such profound revelations.

Burritos in hand, the pair headed to Val's office for some quality strategy time and to take a look at the news. Around ten, they headed to the public library and chatted with patrons and took time to visit with the staff, some of whom had worked for the city for nearly thirty years.

The library was Cambria's central hub, constantly bustling with activity and, quite possibly, the most frequented place in town. Gwen had great rapport with the staff. She'd volunteered for their support organizations for years and developed into a big proponent of area literacy programs. The morning proved busy and positive, a steady stream of Cambrians approached Gwen and reported they'd voted for her. A great way to start the day!

At noon, Val moved Gwen toward the exit, hoping to get her to all appointments on time. Val admired her cousin's commitment to the Cambria's population and, though she hated to tare her away, she sent Gwen to her next round of visits.

The women's business group had an entirely different atmosphere. The group included over one hundred fifty of the most prominent and influential women in town – bankers, real estate agents, city and county government officials, and others representing nearly every industry in town. An old and established group, it tended to be fairly conservative. Many of the women in attendance would be decidedly in Barton's camp, so Val and Gwen had discussed strategy for handling negative comments.

When they arrived, Val saw Kathy Barton in the room and began to doubt their decision to attend. Gwen needed and wanted the support of these women but perhaps after the election was a better time to court them. *Oh well, too late now,* Val thought as they took seats in the middle of the banquet room. Gwen had already chatted with those sitting next to her when Val noticed Kathy heading directly toward them. She nudged Gwen a bit. Gwen looked up in time to greet Barton's wife.

Kathy looked at Val and said, "Ms. Shakely, may I speak with you for a moment?" The tight, tense expression on her face made Val's stomach turn a little. Gwen shot her a warning look as Val stood and followed Kathy to the edge of the room.

Pale and stricken, she turned to Val and said, "I wanted to tell you I'm so very sorry for my husband's behavior." She shifted nervously from one foot to the other, rubbing her hands together as if she was freezing. "Honestly, I don't know what happened to Roger during this campaign. He knows he stepped over a line, and he's lucky you didn't press charges."

Taken off-guard, Val needed a few moments to collect her thoughts. "I admit, Mrs. Barton, your husband scared me to death. I didn't know what he'd do. I've never felt so threatened in my life." Val breathed deeply, and then continued, "I'm grateful for your apology, but I hope you'll understand when I say I never want to have to be around him again."

Shocked at her own honesty as soon as she spoke, Val felt better, relieved. Kathy looked stricken, but continued.

"I want to assure you nothing like that will happen again." She paused, as if wanting to say more, but decided against it. Instead, she turned and walked back to her seat.

When Val returned, Gwen waited anxiously. She'd watched the whole exchange, ready to jump to Val's defense if required. Val filled her in.

"Wow, I wonder if he told her? He must feel fairly bad about it." Gwen sounded shocked.

"I actually feel about a hundred times better. I don't know if he told her or if Constance did, but I feel safer knowing that she knows," Val said.

The guest speaker for the luncheon discussed civic responsibility, and though she didn't specifically discuss the details of the election, she did implore anyone who hadn't yet voted to hit the polls. At the luncheon's end, Gwen spent an hour chatting with some of the ladies. Val returned email queries and moved their afternoon interview to the hotel since they ran a bit behind.

They headed to the Hyatt and got there at the same time as the newspaper reporter. The interview was brief, because they wanted to do a bigger story after the election. The reporter hoped to create some last minute buzz online by posting quotes from both candidates about the importance of voting.

The interview over, Gwen and Val helped prepare the space with the rest of the campaign team. They'd rented two large televisions to place on opposite sides of the hall so guests could mingle and watch the results come in. The catered event had a wine bar set up in one corner.

Guests began filing in around five despite the fact the polls wouldn't close for two hours. Gwen responded to last minute emails and social media posts. She was nothing if not engaged, a diligent and dedicated worker. Val grabbed a glass of wine and found a nice quiet spot to take a break. They'd been moving so fast all day, she hadn't realized how tired she was.

Fifteen minutes before the polls closed, the party shifted into full swing. The crowded ballroom held over two hundred guests who mingled and awaited results. The televisions had been tuned to local election coverage, and the reporters made predictions, reported problems in some precincts, and spoke with election officials.

Right before the polls closed, Gwen stepped up to the podium. "Thank you, everyone, for all your help and support through this process. I've spent the past four years serving this community, and with any luck, I'll get to continue serving you as your mayor." A cheer rose in the crowd.

Val looked around and spied John making his way across the room toward her. Her spirits lifted.

"No matter what happens," Gwen continued, "I want to give thanks to everyone who volunteered countless hours on this campaign. You guys made all the difference. I'd like to thank my campaign manager, Victoria Dunning. I can't tell you how lost I'd be without you, Vicky. And I couldn't have done any of this without the support of Val Shakely. Val, I know politics isn't your cup of tea but you did an amazing job." Val blushed.

John walked up as the audience applauded again and wrapped his arms around Val, whispering in her ear. "She's right, you know." He kissed her cheek and squeezed her tight.

Val smiled at him. "How was your trip?"

"Miserable," he said, but he smiled. "I can't wait to marry you. I did nothing but think about you the whole time." John nuzzled her neck, and Val experienced the usual flood of warmth in her cheeks. She turned and wrapped her arms around him, not even a little self-conscious about the public display of affection.

"I missed you too, handsome." She kissed him deeply, unabashedly, and then realized half the room watched them, wide grins and speculative looks all around.

If the attention wasn't bad enough, Gwen said into the microphone "Oh, and I don't want to take too much credit for it but ... congratulations to Val Shakely and John Hatfield on their engagement!" Gwen's smile looked downright mischievous. Val looked straight at her cousin, smiled, and mouthed, Thanks a lot!" Then she turned back to John and kissed him again for good measure, provoking another round of gasps and whispered comments.

The sound on the televisions was turned up. Results time.

* * *

In anticlimactic fashion, it was over. Gwen's victory over Barton was clean and simple. Colorado's mail-in voting system caused results to be tabulated quickly. By eight, nearly all precincts reported in, and it was revealed that Gwen swept the race with an overwhelming 63% of the votes. Thirty minutes later, news stations reported Barton had officially conceded his position to his opponent.

Gwen even received a brief and strained call from Barton congratulating her on her victory. The celebration, which had begun hours before, ramped up, and it was nearly midnight before Gwen, Val, and the rest of the campaign cleanup crew finally shuffled the last stragglers out the door.

What a wonderful night, Val thought. She had accomplished something amazing for the community. Gwen, beaming, was already discussing her strategies, even though she wouldn't officially take office until the New Year.

John and Val had spent most of the evening tucked away in a corner. They watched the crowd and enjoyed being together once more. A continuous procession of well-wishers came by to congratulate them on their engagement. Val couldn't help but smile knowingly at the conspicuous whispering around the room.

She cuddled closer to John and spent a few blissfully selfish moments reflecting on her luck.

By the time John and Val made it back to her apartment, she was dead on her feet. Her part in the campaign might be over, but Gwen would be up and at 'em early the next morning. Val had already decided to take the day off. With all the hustle and bustle of the last few weeks and especially the last few days, she needed a day full of absolutely nothing. John, having spent the past two days away from Val, didn't want to let her go. He called in sick, and they spent a pleasant couch-potato day together. They ordered pizza, watched movies, and daydreamed about what the future might bring.

CHAPTER 17

In the weeks after the election, Val caught up on client work shuffled aside during the campaign. When she sat down at her desk one Monday, Val prepared to take stock of her career and where she wanted to go. Working on Gwen's campaign had proved an interesting introduction to the world of political campaigning. She didn't know if she'd loved it, though she certainly hadn't hated it as much as she thought she would, at least not the public relations part.

Despite her shy and reserved persona, Val was good at building relationships, a talent that served her well in her profession. She had strong and loyal contacts all over Cambria, and though she rarely wanted to be put in the spotlight, she found it wasn't as uncomfortable as she imagined, at least, once she got used to it.

Notepad in hand, Val brainstormed. She made lists of all the things wanted to do in her personal life, places she'd like to visit and things she'd like to try. She broke down the business into the areas she loved and those she tolerated. Val took a good long look at her lists and pondered what they told her about her life.

She realized the events of the past few weeks had opened her mind to new possibilities. She didn't have to settle for the easy path. She felt less fear. Val wondered how much of this shift in attitude resulted from her relationship with John, and was relieved to recognize the changes within herself had made it possible to be with him.

Val's return to her "normal" life was a time of great introspection and she was determined to take the time to reflect. She met weekly with her therapist and spent nearly every weekend with John and his mother helping to plan the Women's Guild Christmas charity dance. Val loved Anne so much and spending time on this project with her was a treat. Val caught herself from time to time watching John's caring and thoughtful interaction with his mother. It occurred to her his relationship with his mother reflected John's character, and she expressed thanks to have found such a strong and devoted man to spend her life with.

Integrating Val into their family had come naturally and easily for John and his mother. Anne had confided to her son how much she liked the creative energy Val brought to every project and how much she appreciated this quiet, attentive girl. She smiled every time she spied John looking at his beloved.

* * *

Thanksgiving came fast, which proved lucky for Val who barely had a chance to get overly nervous. Not long after the election, John had introduced Val to David, and they'd gotten along swimmingly. David was like the brother Val never had. Now, the time to meet John's sister, June, had arrived.

For some reason, Val felt anxiety about meeting her. The therapist suggested Val's strained relationship with her own sister could have something to do with it. But when June arrived a few days before Thanksgiving, she and Val became immediate friends. June was intelligent and vivacious, and she and Val spent the next few days forging an unbreakable bond.

Val's mom and sister came the day before Thanksgiving. John and Val picked them up at the airport, and while Val's mother immediately took to John, Liz seemed more reserved. After an awkward ride to Cambria, Val realized the years of estrangement had been particularly hard on her sister. It would take time to make things right between them.

Seeing the families together over the holiday was like witnessing a miracle. Val's family, broken beyond anyone's realization after her father's death, was reborn. The two families coming together seemed to bridge gaps that had kept Val, her mother, and sister from being a real family for nearly a decade. Val found much needed common ground with her sister. By the weekend, the farewells were tearful, and for the first time in a long time, Val was whole. Connected.

After dropping her family at the airport, John and Val settled in for one of many quiet nights at home. Content. Loved.

* * *

The Grand Ballroom at the Cambria Cultural Museum looked sparkling and surreal. Holiday décor abounded. Like in a dream, glittering garlands swept through the air, red bursts of holly berries and poinsettias in every direction. A huge dance floor occupied the middle of the ballroom with tables and chairs all around, centerpieces overflowed with holiday cheer.

Val and Gwen arrived for the Christmas ball a little after seven. John escorted his mother, as he did every year. Val scanned the room for him as they made their way toward the bar. Wine glasses in hand, Val and Gwen toasted their last night out before Gwen's inauguration.

"It's absolutely breathtaking in here," Gwen murmured, taking in all the warmth and holiday cheer.

Val had spent countless hours in the preceding days assisting with decorations. Nonetheless, she still experienced amazement at the final effect. Lights dimmed, spotlights caught every sparkly thing in the room. The scene looked like something out of an old Hollywood holiday movie. And the guests, increasing in numbers every minute, had dressed exquisitely for the occasion.

Gwen had chosen a simple, floor length emerald green gown and was the picture of elegance and sophistication. Val had taken the opportunity to live out a childhood fantasy. She'd ordered a red velvet ball gown with a sweeping princess neckline that reminded her of one of her favorite movie scenes – the Christmas dance in *Meet Me in St. Louis*. She felt glamorous and beautiful, and she'd kept her wardrobe choice under wraps, hoping to surprise John.

Val's hair was pinned up in shining curls, exposing her neck. Soon, she sensed John's familiar and exhilarating warm breath as he leaned in close to tenderly kiss the bare skin. She smiled warmly and turned around. As she twirled, her dress spun out with her, creating exactly the effect she'd imagined it would. John took in every inch of and smiled with a goofy, dreamlike expression.

"You look amazing in that tux, handsome," Val teased, reaching up to kiss him on the cheek.

With her face still near his, he whispered into her ear, "Every time I think I've seen you at your most beautiful ..." His voice trailed off as he brushed his lips across her cheek. He could feel the heat radiating from their blushing, and he lingered with his face near hers while he wrapped his arms around the woman he'd marry. The woman he loved more than he could have imagined loving another person.

"Oh, Val, you look magnificent," Anne said as she approached from another direction. John moved to give Val room to respond, but kept his arms firmly wrapped around her, unwilling to let go.

"It's so unbelievably beautiful in here, Anne!" Val's face filled with delight. "Even seeing it yesterday, I wouldn't have imagined it could be so ... It's like a fantasy." She finally broke apart from John long enough to give her dress another quick twirl and bask in the dreaminess of the occasion.

Anne turned to Gwen, "Madame Mayor, could I borrow you for a moment?" She whisked Gwen away for photo ops.

Val and John looked for empty seats somewhere to cuddle and kiss without feeling too conspicuous. The room had filled to near capacity, and they ended up seated near the center of the room right in front of the dance floor. The Women's Guild had hired a huge Big Band-style ensemble, and they played fantastically. The dance floor was lively with elegant couples swinging each other to the music. Val enjoyed herself so much she didn't even notice Gwen return to sit next to them.

"Roger Barton looks happier than I've ever seen him," Gwen remarked as she sat down. Then, with a snarky grin on her face, she added, "almost human."

Val looked out into the dancing couples, following Gwen's eyes, and experienced a shock when she realized one of the couples was Roger and Kathy Barton. Barton looked ten years younger beaming at his wife.

"He looks relieved," Val noted. It seemed Barton had ended up in a better place after losing the election, and she wondered how much stress had gotten to him. Despite her dislike for Barton, she couldn't help feeling bad for him. His behavior during the election had gone over the top, and she was relieved to see him looking normal again.

Gwen said, "I spoke with him yesterday. He's stepping out of politics. Seems his wife laid down the law after the election and made him promise to focus on his business for a while and then retire. I think she's had enough."

"It looks like the decision was a good one," Val said, smiling at the happy expression on Kathy's face. Val had long since forgiven Barton for his attack. Seeing him twirl his wife on the dance floor seemed to prove the crazy erratic anger of his political days was a thing of the past. In the meantime, Val learned to stand up for herself. She'd even enrolled in a self-defense class so she'd never end up in the same vulnerable position again without a way to get out of it. She returned her attention to Gwen, ready to put Barton behind her once and for all.

Gwen stared at the dancers and looked wistful. So absorbed by the motion on the dance floor, she didn't notice the tall, sandy blond stranger walk up beside her. Val looked up and tried to recognize the man who'd taken a position right next to Gwen and cleared his throat repeatedly in an attempt to get her attention. Val gave Gwen a nudge, taking pity on the poor, dashing gentleman.

Gwen looked up, and a smile broke out across her face. "Jason!" she exclaimed, jumping up to greet him.

Genuinely perplexed, Val wracked her brain trying to figure out who Jason was. Gwen turned, seeing the confused look on her cousin's face and giggled. She put on her best official voice and said, "Val? John? This is Jason Turri." Val stood to shake hands with the mystery man and noticed John's broad and knowing smile. Finally, she realized Jason was the man John had talked to at the debate.

Gwen continued, "Jason works for the city, and we kept running into one another, first professionally and then ..." She paused to smile mischievously. "I think he started stalking me." Her voice was ripe with excitement.

Val looked at Jason and then at John, who didn't look the least bit surprised. John said, "Jason and I have been friends since high school, and, um, we've collaborated on a few projects here and there." Jason shot John a warning look, but his expression remained playful and positive.

"Now, now. Don't give away all my secrets until I've been properly introduced. It's nice to finally meet you, Val. Between Gwen and John, I feel I've known you for years." Val smiled and took a moment to give Jason a once over. He was gorgeous with stunning green eyes and sandy hair. And the goofy smile on Gwen's face gave away her feelings for him. Val shot Gwen a quizzical look, and Gwen mouthed, "Later."

"What secrets?" Gwen asked, sidling up against Jason

Jason took a tentative breath. "I'm Jabber."

Watching Gwen's face as she reacted to the news resembled watching a movie in fast forward. In a matter of seconds, she went from shocked to smiling, with a whole lot in between.

"You rat! You leaked the travel audit information. Do you know how much trouble you got me into!" Then Gwen paused. "Wait, do you know how much trouble you could have gotten *yourself* into? You're a city employee, for goodness sake!" Gwen smiled but Val knew from the tone of her voice she was stressed.

"I know, that's why I've always kept my identity a secret," Jason replied. He held his hands out to Gwen in a sign of surrender. "Now that we're together, I'm feeling a little guilty about all the comments on your looks."

John chuckled. "Yeah, you probably should've kept this little revelation under wraps."

"Nah. Now that I'm dating the mayor, I've got enough on my plate without continuing Jabber. As of tonight, I'm retired. That's part of the reason I came clean."

Val continued to be shocked by this new turn of events, but Gwen had already regained her composure.

"I believe I have enough ammo on you now to get us through the next century." Gwen winked at Jason, and he sighed, obviously relieved at Gwen's good nature and acceptance.

Jason turned to John. "Looks like we're out of business, buddy." He grinned. "It's been an interesting ride." John simply smiled and wrapped his arm around Val's shoulders. She relaxed into his side thinking, *well it's not the weirdest thing that's happened to me in the last few weeks.*

Returning his attention to Gwen, Jason held out a hand and said, "Would you like to dance, Madame Mayor?" Gwen took his hand and, giggling like a teenager, headed to the dance floor.

"I wonder how long that's been going on?" John asked, watching them dance.

"Um, I honestly have no idea. I don't remember her ever having mentioned Jason, even in passing. Though now that I think about it, I remember them talking at Mavis Bean's party." Val studied her cousin. Gwen had always been an open book. "They make a dazzling couple."

"Not half so dazzling as you and I," John grinned, glad Val seemed to be taking this all in stride. He offered Val his hand, "May I have this dance, love?"

Val put her hand in his, and he led her onto the dance floor. The band played a jazzy version of *It Had to Be You*, and John pulled Val in close, swaying to the music and singing along softly in her ear. For a moment, her mind wandered. She thought about her father and his ups and downs.

She remembered a Christmas when, as a little girl, her father had turned on holiday music and danced around the room with Val standing on his feet. It was a joyful moment, and though she remembered it fondly, Val realized those happy moments with her dad had been few and far between.

"Val?" John's voice brought her back into the moment.

"Mmm?" She murmured.

"I want to tell you something," he said. Val looked into his dark, intense eyes and waited. He leaned forward and whispered. "I love you. I will love you forever." And, tenderly cradling Val's face in his hands, John kissed her.

The band continued playing, and John and Val made their way around the dance floor, completely immersed in one another. The evening was perfect, and for the first time in a long time, Val looked forward to her future.

The *"Serious About Writing"* Publishing Package

Are you interested in publishing your fiction or non-fiction title with the prestige of an imprint? Do you want a staff of editors and designers to provide the best quality product possible? Is it important to keep your copyright and all profits from your book sales? Oh, and would you like it done in three months instead of the typical 18 months to two years required by a traditional publisher?

Look into our *"Serious About Writing"* package. We don't take commissions and don't give advances. We review your manuscript regardless if it's sent by you or by an agent. In exchange for an up-front one-time fee, we make sure your work is in the best shape possible and receives the acceptance it deserves.

Here are just some of the advantages:

- Expert editing and design staff.
- Personal service throughout all aspects of the process.
- Prestige of a third-party publisher.
- Distribution to Amazon, Kindle, and other outlets.
- Creation of ISBN & bar code.
- Retention of all copyrights.
- One hundred percent royalties.
- Completion and publication within 90 days.
- A marketing plan that can be implemented by the author.

You can choose multiple avenues to accomplish these same tasks, or take advantage of the *"Serious About Writing"* package. Contact us for more information at woodenpantspub@gmail.com. You can also visit our website, woodenpantspub.com, and fill out the form on the Publication page. We look forward to working with you toward your goal of author entrepreneurship!

Made in the USA
San Bernardino, CA
25 August 2016